Story of O

Also by Pauline Réage
Published by Grove Press

Return to the Château: Story of O, Part 2

Story of O

by
Pauline Réage

Translated from the French by
Sabine d'Estrée

Preface by Jean Paulhan
of the Académie Française

A Note on Story of O by
André Pieyre de Mandiargues

GROVE PRESS, INC.   NEW YORK

Originally published in Paris, France,
Chez Jean-Jacques Pauvert in 1954, as
Histoire d'O, copyright © 1954 by
Jean-Jacques Pauvert

"A Note on Story of O" was published in
Le Belvédère, Paris, France, Bernard Grasset
Editeur,
Copyright © 1958 by Editions Bernard Grasset

Eighteenth Printing 1978
ISBN: 0-394-17143-8
Grove Press ISBN: 0-8021-4169-2
Library of Congress Catalog Card Number:
66-13262

Manufactured in the United States of America

Distributed by Random House, Inc., New York

GROVE PRESS, INC., 196 West Houston Street,
New York, N.Y. 10014

Contents

Translator's Note

In July of 1954, one of the most curious—and mysterious—novels of recent times appeared under the imprint of a young French publisher, Jean-Jacques Pauvert: *Histoire d'O* [*Story of O*]. Its author was Pauline Réage, a name completely unknown in French literary circles, where everyone knows everyone. The work was greeted with considerable respect by the critics, who none the less clearly did not know what to make of this latter-day, female Sade. Part of their circumspection no doubt derived from the fact that Jean Paulhan, himself a leading writer, critic, editor, and now member of the august *Académie Française*,[1] wrote a Preface to the book in the form of an

---

[1] There is a story, perhaps apocryphal, that when M. Paulhan was nominated for *l'Académie Française*, opponents to his candidacy placed a copy of the yellow-covered volume of *O* on the chair of each of the Academy members. Another version has it that the copies were so placed by members promoting his candidacy, who claimed that his discovery of and Preface to *O* constituted another proof of his literary acumen. Whatever the truth, M. Paulhan was promptly elected as one of France's forty immortals.

essay entitled "Happiness in Slavery," which, however sympathetic, hardly helped to clarify any of the mystery surrounding the work.

During the winter following its publication, *Story of O* became the talk of the French salons and cafés. Even in Paris, where scandal is slow to ignite, there was an element of shock in these exchanges—that such a book, such a total anachronism, could appear, full-blown, in the mid-twentieth century. But the real interest centered around the mystery: who was Pauline Réage? Until her identity was bared, people found it difficult to assume a reasonable stance vis-à-vis the work: if Pauline Réage was the pseudonym of some eminent writer, they would feel compelled to react one way; if she were a complete unknown, another; and if indeed she were a literary hack merely seeking notoriety, then still another.

The mystery entered a new phase when, in February, 1955, the book was awarded the *Prix des Deux Magots*—a prize established for and generally awarded to new works of an unconventional nature, which counted highly respected novelists Raymond Queneau and Antoine Blondin among its laureates. At this point, the newspapers seized on the book—and the mystery—and headlines blared the news to the general public. Inevitably, the sanctity of the general public being menaced, the police moved in. Although there was never any official notification that an investigation was under way, numerous personalities, including Messrs. Paulhan and Pauvert, were interrogated. But suddenly, as unofficially as it had begun, the investigation ceased. It is said that the desist order was sent down by a high government official, but this remains unsubstantiated. In any event, there have never been any further censorship problems.

To this day, no one knows who Pauline Réage is. In his Preface, Paulhan speculates that the author is a woman, citing as evidence not only the uncommon attention to details of dress and make-up, but that telling scene in which O, abandoned by her lover, René, to the torments and tortures of his Roissy colleagues, still has the (feminine) presence of mind to notice that René's slippers are worn and frayed, and to note in her mind that she must buy him another pair.

I have never met Pauline Réage, although, through questions of the translation, I have been in indirect communication (via the French publisher, Jean-Jacques Pauvert), and received the author's comments. I trust I am not betraying a confidence, or appearing immodest, when I say that the author has gone out of her way to say how pleased she is with those portions of the translation she has read. I long puzzled over this unusual display of literary generosity on the part of an author concerning a translator, and only recently did I discover, or suspect I had discovered, the reason for it. There exists an earlier translation of O, made in Paris several years ago. I trust I shall not be accused of a corresponding lack of generosity if I say (and I am not the first, and far from the only one, to say it) that this earlier version is less a translation than an adaptation. It reads somehow as though the adapter-translator were in fact embarrassed by the work: certain parts are glossed over; whole descriptions, nonexistent in the original, are written in; and, indeed, much of the book is paraphrased rather than translated directly. As one who had read the work in French when it first appeared, and admired not only its contents but the extreme felicity of the style, what troubled me most about the earlier English version was its seeming disdain for this obvious style. Subsequently, I learned this translator was a man, and it seemed to me that this fact alone sufficed to explain both the embarrassment—*male* embarrassment—manifest in his version, and also why Pauline Réage had gone out of her way to comment favorably on mine: *Story of O*, written by a woman, demands a woman translator, one who will humble herself before the work and be satisfied simply to render it, as faithfully as possible, without interpretation or unwanted elaboration. Faced with a work such as *O*, male pride, male superiority—however liberal the male, however much he may try to suppress them—will, I am certain, somehow intrude. Like O, therefore, I have tried to humble myself, to remain as faithful as possible (although, if the reader will forgive, I have attempted to stop short of slavishness) to the intent and style of the author.

Story of O is the work of an original writer, who has dared to present us with certain truths, or intimations of truth, rarely found in literature. However much one may disagree with, or even profoundly dislike, these truths (or, if you will, these ideas), Pauline Réage has done what all good artists aim for and, when they are successful, accomplish: to arouse us from the lethargy of our set ways and routine lives, prick us into consciousness, provoke a reaction (whether positive or negative, it matters little) within us; in short, to make us think. That in itself is a rare enough occurrence so that we should be grateful indeed whenever we have the good fortune to encounter it.

M. Paulhan, in speculating about the book's conclusion, suggests that the author may have permitted herself this one small indulgence—the end—with the thought in mind of one day continuing O's adventures. To date, however, no sequel has been forthcoming, and the present work, with its many mysteries still unsolved, is all we have.[2] For beyond the more or less general consensus that the author is a woman, nothing is certain about the work. And yet, perhaps there is a kind of virtue in this, for we are thus obliged to judge the book itself, uncluttered by any outside considerations. Like O before her judges, the work stands naked and alone.

S. d'E.

---

[2] Or, to be exact, almost all. A year or two after *O* appeared, Miss Réage wrote the preface to another somewhat mysterious work entitled *l'Image*, by Jean de Berg, which was published in 1956 by *Les Editions de Minuit*, the publishers of most of the avant-garde fiction in France since World War II. Since then, however, she has not been heard from again.

A Note on Story of O

by André Pieyre de Mandiargues

Apropos of *Story of O* (the object of a notoriety which its author, Madame Pauline Réage or whoever is hiding behind that mask of a perfect little girl—and she is most assuredly a woman—doubtless neither expected nor desired), people are going about—both those who have read the book and those who have as yet been unable to find a copy of the yellow-jacketed work—trying to outdo one another by asserting that it is an "erotic" book. The formula is familiar, too quickly and too easily employed. It would not be a bad idea, in this case as in others, to consider it from the vantage point of time, which is a convenient position when one finds oneself in the uncomfortable situation of having to judge an object so close at hand and so unusual that it tends to blind you.

Now, it seems fairly obvious that the time of a work of

fiction, both in plot and continuity, is always a kind of past, whether or not the author likes it, whereas the time of (physical) love is specifically the present. If we accept the fact that the art of lovers, as the saying goes, is to make pleasure last as long as possible, then it is a question of a multitude of splendid and excruciating moments with neither past nor future, quite independent of one another, although they all are rather alike. The rough comparison between an alternating and a direct current is not to be discarded. Making allowances for the florid language, one might also say of lovers that they cull pleasure like a string of pearls. And when a novelist, or a writer of fiction, attempts through his narrative to re-create the fleeting intensity of these precious moments, to set them squarely before the eyes of the reader in order to arouse his senses, if his work is truly erotic it will unfold as a series of repetitious sequences punctuated here and there on rare occasions by sudden shifts of fortune which have nothing to do with the central, sensual fact, but without which the work would be unreadable. Most of the novels of Sade, and the Grandiose *Trois filles et leur mère* by Pierre Louÿs, are examples of this sort.

Faced with these or with other more recent works whose purpose, whether avowed or not, is fairly obvious, since everything, from plot to language, contributes to the goal of voluptuousness—*Story of O* is not, strictly speaking, an erotic book. In fact, of the two planes on which it is constructed, that of the mind (or rather: the soul) ruthlessly dominates that of the flesh. The picture that the four long chapters give of the modern world, the action, the characters, are all extraordinarily vivid; above all, they are not dependent upon the sensual fire as they would be in an erotic book. Here we are dealing with a genuine novel, one we should not hesitate to categorize as a mystic work.

For, beneath the guise and methods of eroticism, the subject is the tragic flowering of a woman in the abdication of her freedom, in willful slavery, in humiliation, in the prostitution imposed upon her by her masters, in torture, and even in the death which, after she has suffered every other ignominy, she requests and they agree to.

It was rightly said of Sade that his is the work of a moralist. Erotic books are almost all alike in this respect: either they are working toward the elaboration of a revolutionary morality, or they echo the morality of their age, against which they are protesting. But women are little given to these Aristotelian speculations. And Pauline Réage is as completely devoid of morality as is the Portuguese Nun or Saint Therese of Avila.

The reader may be surprised by our use of the term "flowering." Is the term apt? I think it is. In any event, what we are shown in *Story of O* is a complete spiritual transformation, what others would call an *ascesis*. Madame Réage, who has a good knowledge of English and does not mind showing it, could have entitled her book: *A Woman's Progress*.

That this book, which is anything but vulgar, owes a debt to the sort of productions commonly found in catalogues of vile pornography, is indeed surprising; but it is also true. In the same way that Julien Gracq, in his preface to *Au Château d'Argol*, declaring that all battles are won or lost according to the same plans, voluntarily limited his instruments of terror to the arsenal of the Gothic novels of the end of the eighteenth and beginning of the nineteenth century, so Madame Réage uses the tried-and-true formulas of more than a hundred volumes sold under the counter. The black leather, the little wasp-waisted corsets, the whips and riding crops, the rooms sound-proofed to muffle the cries, the brandings with a red-hot iron, the intimate rings and chains: there is nothing here so original that we have not already encountered it in *Unwilling Slaves, Infernal Voluptuousness;* in *Sonia the Domineering* or *Sonia Defeated;* in *Slavery,* in *The Ardent Tutelage,* in *Hot Days,* or in the *Slaves of John Krissler.* . . . And if Pauline Réage, whose ability to construct a story is, as I have said, that of a very great novelist, thus refuses to exercise her imagination when dwelling on details, there is good reason to believe that it is a matter of pride, that she wishes to glory in triumphing through methods which are in the public domain. It has been noted that the owl costume O wears in the last chapter is actually like a mask by Leonor Fini, whose sensual and disturbing qualities I had occasion to comment upon not long ago. Madame Réage has seized upon this cast-off piece of clothing for a masked ball and has infused it with a prodigious and sinister life; through an act of admirable intuition, she has understood the role for which it was suited, and then follows the major scene at the end, when O is exposed to public scorn: the display of a body which is no longer anything but an object, flouted beneath the plumage, offered to the first comer. Then: death. Inevitably; woman, through the decline of her flesh, having become pure spirit.

Yes, *Story of O,* as I have said, is indeed a mystic book! Proud Réage . . . In the midst of her glowing tale, she has a way of involving herself, of slipping, at the worst possible moments, into the skin of her heroine, which is enough to make one shudder and at the same time make one feel a certain tenderness for her. The way one would feel toward a brave bull who has fought well. The château at Roissy, like the bull ring, is the sacrificial site. When women become exasperated, they sometimes assume postures wherein they seem to be offering themselves to the arrows of misfortune, and it would not be difficult to draw from them, for the sake of youth, some sublime examples. For it is difficult to go as far down as Réage does, under cover of the mask and of night but beneath the cruelest light, and she reaches depths of humiliation which have scarcely been plumbed by Genet, or by Adamov in the terrible pages of his *L'Epreuve*. With her, not the faintest trace of dilettantism. Still proudly, the black pact is candidly accepted, and carried through to its ultimate consequences. It is in this, perhaps, that she differs especially from the authors of erotic books, almost all of whom have known how to keep themselves aloof by keeping to the privileged terrain of dandyism, by torturing victims with whom they are unfamiliar, by using humor and imagination, by discreetly keeping exits open by which, at dawn, they can leave, without having overly sullied or compromised themselves.

Such a descent into hell, of which the rightful issue is the destruction of the body (and it is O's fanatic wish that her body be insulted, then destroyed), has raised the question of "masochism." The word, first of all, is detestable, deriving from one of the worst, most stupid, and ridiculous writers of the second half of the nineteenth century. *Venus in Furs* was all the rage. Who, unless he were a trifle addle-brained, would still have any interest in this empty prattle? Who would dare to compare it with the great, heavy silence cast like a cape over O's tortures? As for the passion, or vice, which the term designates, we can at most allot it a minor role in Pauline Réage's book, for it is so completely overwhelmed by the heroine's ardor, transfigured by a current which comes from the soul and not from the body, and which in fact is directed against the body.

Jean Paulhan, in his ingeniously arranged Preface, tells

us that erotic books—Réage's book—are dangerous. This is an understatement, and it is my opinion that there is much more seductive virtue in *Story of O* than in the others. Because innocent souls (if there are any) have an unreasoned but keen taste for suffering, and nothing seduces them so easily as does the view of a martyr. And also because the innocent souls (assuming, also, that they know how to read) will at first glance be put off by the coarse vocabulary of classical erotology, whereas they will find all sorts of allurements in Pauline Réage's writing, which is incredibly decent in relation to the subjects dealt with. If the writing is not the foremost quality of the book, it is certainly not the least: pure as the writing of the *Princesse de Clèves*, warm as . . . I shall refrain from saying what, and of a simple density which emphasizes, or provokes, the movements of the heart. Her writing offers an example, which will not be heeded in an age when writers, following the perfidious example of Céline, have a tendency to use indiscriminately erotic or scatological language, which when used legitimately, can be extremely beautiful and effective.

Shall we one day see on the finger of some woman the formidable iron ring which strips the person wearing it of her freedom, since she places her body at the disposal of all those who are able to read the insignia engraved in the setting? And, what is especially important, shall we be able to tell which one is Pauline Réage? Probably not. But already Baudelaire is offering his hand to her, the Portuguese Nun is approaching her a trifle timidly, the Nun of Dülmen is ready to open her arms to her, and she is about to enter that small circle of blessed and accursed creatures which constitutes the only aristocracy which one can consider today with any degree of respect.

Happiness in Slavery

by Jean Paulhan

of l'Académie Française

A Revolt in Barbados

In the course of the year 1838, the peaceful island of
Barbados was rocked by a strange and bloody revolt.
About two hundred Negroes of both sexes, all of whom
had recently been emancipated by the Proclamations of
March, came one morning to beg their former master, a
certain Glenelg, to take them back into bondage. An Anabaptist minister, acting as spokesman for the group, read

out a list of grievances which he had compiled and recorded in a notebook. Then the discussion began. But Glenelg, either from timidity or because he was scrupulous, or simply afraid of the law, refused to be swayed. At which point he was at first mildly jostled, then set upon and massacred, together with his family, by the Negroes, who that same evening repaired to their cabins, their palavers, their labors, and customary rituals. Swift action on the part of Governor MacGregor succeeded in suppressing the matter, and the emancipation pursued its course. As for the notebook of grievances, it has never been recovered.

There are times when I think of that notebook. It is quite likely that it contained, aside from the justified complaints concerning the organization of the workhouses, the substitution of cell for lash, and the rule making it illegal for the "apprentices"—for such were the newly-freed workers called—to fall ill, it is likely that it contained at least the rough draft of an apologia for slavery. The remark, for instance, that the only freedoms we really appreciate are those which cast others into an equivalent state of servitude. There is not a man alive who thanks his lucky stars for the privilege of being able to breathe freely. But if, for example, I obtain permission to play the banjo merrily till two in the morning, my neighbor loses the right *not* to hear me play till two in the morning. If I manage to get along without working, my neighbor has to work for two. And, what is more, we know how an all-consuming passion for freedom in the world never fails to lead to conflicts and wars which are no less consuming. Add to this the fact that, since the slave, according to at least one dialectic, is in turn destined to become the master, then we would doubtless be wrong to precipitate the natural order of events. Finally, let it be said that to surrender oneself to the will of others (as often happens with lovers and mystics) and so find oneself at last rid of selfish pleasures, interests, and personal complexes, is in no wise a joyless act, nor one lacking in grandeur. In short, this notebook would seem even more heretical today than it did some hundred and thirty years ago: today it would be considered a dangerous book.

What we are concerned with here is another kind of dangerous book. To be more specific: with an erotic book.

I. —Decisive as a letter

Why, in fact, are they called dangerous? A somewhat risky business, to say the least. For since there is courage in numbers, the very act of referring to them as such would seem bound to make us want to read them and expose ourselves to the danger. And it is with good reason that geographical societies warn their members that, whenever they are relating their adventures, they should avoid dwelling overly on the dangers they have encountered. It is not a question of modesty, but rather of not leading anyone else into temptation (witness the ease with which wars are begun). But what dangers?

From where I stand, there is at least one danger I can easily perceive. It is a modest danger. From every indication, *Story of O* is one of those books which marks the reader, which leaves him not quite, or not at all, the same as he was before he read it. Such books are strangely involved with the influence they exert, changing in accordance with that influence. After a few years, they are no longer the same books, and consequently the initial reviewers soon seem to have been a bit simple-minded. But that cannot be helped, a reviewer should never be afraid to make a fool of himself. With this thought in mind, the simplest thing for me to do is admit that I hardly know what to make of it, or what it all means. I advance through O with a strange feeling, as though I am moving through a fairy tale—we know that fairy tales are erotic novels for children—through one of those fairy castles which appears abandoned, and yet the armchairs in their slip covers and the ottomans and the four-poster beds are all neatly dusted, and the whips and riding crops are too: they are, if I may say so, dusted by definition. Not a speck of rust on the chains or a trace of steam on the multicolored windowpanes. If there is one word which comes to mind when I think of O, that word is *decency*. It is a word which would be far too difficult for me to try and justify, so I shall not even try. And then this wind which blows endlessly, through all the rooms. In O, there also blows some indefinable, always pure and violent spirit, endless and unadulterated. It is a decisive spirit which nothing disturbs, whether it be moans or horrors, ecstasy or nausea. And, if I must make another confession, this type of thing is not, generally speaking, my cup of tea. I incline to works in which the author is hesitant, indicating by some show of embarrassment that he was at first intimidated by his subject, that there were moments when he doubted he would ever be able to bring it off. But from beginning to end, the story of O is managed rather like some brilliant feat. It reminds you more of a speech than a mere effusion; of a letter rather than a secret diary. But to whom is the letter addressed? Whom is the speech trying to convince? Whom can we ask? I don't even know who you are.

That you are a woman I have little doubt. Not so much because of the kind of detail you delight in describing—the green satin dresses, wasp-waist corsets, and skirts rolled up a number of turns (like hair rolled up in a curler)—but rather because of something like this: the day when René abandons O to still further torments, she still manages to have enough presence of mind to notice that her lover's slippers are frayed, and notes that she will have to buy him another pair. To me, such a thought seems almost unimaginable. It is something a man would never have thought of, or at least would never have dared express.

And yet, in her own way O expresses a virile ideal. Virile, or at least masculine. At last a woman who admits it! Who admits what? Something that women have always refused till now to admit (and today more than ever before). Something that men have always reproached them with: that they never cease obeying their nature, the call of their blood, that everything in them, even their minds, is sex. That they have constantly to be nourished, constantly washed and made up, constantly beaten. That all they need is a good master, one who is not too lax or kind: for the moment we make any show of tenderness they draw upon it, turning all the zest, joy, and character at their command to make others love them. In short, that we must, when we go to see them, take a whip along. Rare is the man who has not dreamed of possessing Justine. But, so far as I know, no woman has ever dreamed of *being* Justine. I mean, dreamed aloud, with this same pride at being grieved and in tears, this consuming violence, with this voracious capacity for suffering, and this amazing will, stretched to the breaking point, and even beyond. Woman you may be, but descended from a knight, or a crusader. As though yours was a dual personality, or the person for whom your letter was intended was so constantly present that you borrowed his taste, and his voice. But what kind of woman, and who are you?

In any event, the story of O has deep roots. It has, in my opinion, that feeling of repose, of spaciousness as it were, which one finds only in a tale which the author has nurtured within her for a long time: a tale with which she is wholly familiar. Who is Pauline Réage? Is she—for there are such people—a mere dreamer? (It is enough, they say, to listen to the dictates of your heart. It is a heart that nothing can dissuade.) Is she a woman of the world, who knows whereof she speaks? Who knows whereof she speaks and is astonished that an adventure that began with such promise—or at least with such sobriety, in a climate of asceticism and chastisement—should turn out so badly and end on a note of dubious smugness, for, it seems generally to be agreed, O remains in that kind of brothel to which she was led by love; and not only does she remain there, she rather likes it. And yet, in this connection:

II. —A ruthless decency

I too was surprised by the end. And nothing you can say will convince me it is the real end. That in reality (so to speak) your heroine convinces Sir Stephen to consent to her death. He will remove her irons only after she is dead. But, obviously, there are things that have been left unsaid, and that busy little bee—I am referring to Pauline Réage—has kept part of the honey for herself. Who knows, perhaps this once she let herself be seduced by a writer's concern: that she might one day want to write a sequel to O's adventures. Besides, that ending is so obvious it was hardly worth stating. We discover it without any trouble. We discover it, and somehow it obsesses us. But you, the author, how did you think it up—and what is the open sesame which explains it? I keep harping on this because I feel certain that once it has been found, then the ottomans and the four-posters, and even the chains will be explained and will allow this tall, dim figure, this scheming phantom, these curious breaths of air, to move freely to and fro among them.

At this point I must pause and consider what there is about masculine desire which is in fact strange and indefensible. We hear of those formations of rocks which suddenly shift when the winds blow upon them, or else emit a soughing sound or give forth a mandolin-like music. People come from near and far to see them. And yet one's initial impulse is to turn and run from such phenomena, no matter how much one may love music. Actually, what if the role of the erotic (or of dangerous books, if you prefer) was to inform and instruct us? To reassure us on the subject, the way a father confessor does? I realize that, in general, people grow accustomed to it. Nor do men remain embarrassed for very long. They make up their minds, they claim that they were the ones who started it all. They are lying and, if I may say so, the facts are clear: obvious, too obvious.

Women do too, I shall be told. No doubt they do, but with them the act is not visible. They can always say that they're not. How decent! Whence no doubt derives the notion that women are the more beautiful of the two, that beauty is feminine. More beautiful, I'm not so sure. But more discreet in any case, less obvious, and this is a kind of beauty. I have twice now alluded to the idea of decency with respect to a book in which decency is hardly the question. . . .

But is it true that decency is hardly germane here? I am not thinking of that kind of colorless, hypocritical decency which limits itself to dissimulation, which flees from the presence of the stone and denies having seen it move. There is another kind of decency, indomitable and quick to punish, a decency which humbles the flesh sufficiently to render it its original integrity, which by force returns it to the days when desire had not been made manifest and the rocks had not yet sung. A decency into whose hands it is dangerous to fall. For, to satisfy it, nothing less than the hands tied behind the back will do, than the knees spread apart and bodies spread-eagled, than sweat and tears.

I seem to be saying frightful things. Perhaps I am, but in that case terror is our daily bread—and perhaps dangerous books are those which restore us to our natural state of danger. What lover would not be terrified if he were to weigh for one moment the full implication of his declaration, which is not made lightly, to commit himself for life? And what mistress, if she were to measure for a moment the meaning of her words: "Before I met you I have never loved anyone else. . . . I have never experienced real emotion before I knew you?" would not be equally terror-stricken at the words slipping past her lips? Or these, more sagacious—sagacious?—: "I should like to punish myself for having been happy before I met you!" There she is, trapped by her own words. There she is, so to speak, getting what she asked for.

Thus, in the story of *O*, there is no lack of torture. There is no lack of flogging, with a riding crop, or even of branding with a red-hot iron, not to mention the leather collar and the spectacle on the terrace. Almost as many tortures as there are prayers in the life of ascetics in the desert. No less carefully distinguished, and as though numbered—separated one from the other by little stones. They are not always joyous tortures—I mean inflicted joyfully. René refuses to inflict any, and although Sir Stephen consents to them, it is as though he is performing a duty. So far as we can tell, they do not enjoy themselves. There is nothing sadistic about them. It all happens as though it were O alone who, from the outset, demanded to be chastised, to be forced in her retreats.

At this point some fool is going to mention masochism. I don't mind, but all it will do is to add a false mystery to the real one, a mystery of semantics pure and simple. What does masochism mean? That pain is at the same time pleasure, that suffering is also joy? That may well be. These are the kind of affirmations widely used by metaphysicians—who are also prone to proclaim that all absence is presence, all speech silence—and let me be the last one to deny that these declarations may indeed have their meaning (though one I do not understand), or at least their usefulness. But it is a usefulness that does not, in any event, derive from simple observation—and is therefore not the concern of doctors or mere psychologists and, all the more so, of simpletons or fools. "No," I can hear someone saying to me, "while we are dealing here with pain, it is a pain the masochist is capable of transforming into pleasure; a suffering which he, by some secret alchemy he alone possesses, can turn into pure joy."

What a wonderful piece of news! At last man has discovered what he has been searching for so doggedly through the ages, in medicine, ethics, philosophy, and religion: the means to avoid pain—or at least to transcend it, to understand it (were it only by seeing therein the effect of our stupidity or mistakes). What is more, man might easily have made this discovery in ages past, for in truth masochists are not a recent invention. And so I am amazed that this discovery was not greeted by a great fanfare and bestowal of signal honors; that no attempt was made to steal the secret. And I'm also surprised that these masochists were not rounded up and herded into the laboratories and museums, in cages, the better to be observed and studied.

Perhaps men never pose themselves any questions which have not already been answered. Perhaps it would be enough to get them together to wrest them from their solitude (as though it were not some purely visionary, human desire). Well, here at least is the cage, and here is this young woman in the cage. All we have to do now is listen to her.

III. —Strange love letter

She says: "You shouldn't be surprised. Take a closer look at your love. It would be terrified if it realized for one moment that I'm a woman, and alive. And it is not by ignoring the fiery wellsprings of the blood that you will dry them up.

"Your jealousy does not deceive you. It is true that you make me healthy and happy and a thousand times more alive. Yet there is nothing I can do to prevent this happiness from turning against you. The stone also sings more loudly when the blood flows free and the body is at rest. Keep me rather in this cage, and feed me sparingly, if you dare. Anything that brings me closer to illness and the edge of death makes me more faithful. It is only when you make me suffer that I feel safe and secure. You should never have agreed to be a god for me if you were afraid to assume the duties of a god, and we all know that they are not as tender as all that. You have already seen me cry. Now you must learn to relish my tears. And my neck: is it not charming when, filled with a moan I am striving to stifle, it grows tense and contorted in spite of my attempts to control it? It is all too true that when you come to call on us, you should bring a whip along. And, for more than one among us, a cat-o'-nine-tails."

She hastens to add: "That joke is in such poor taste! But the fact is you've missed the whole point. And if I were not so madly in love with you, do you think I would dare to speak to you in this way? and betray my peers?"

She adds: "What constantly betrays you is my imagination, my vague dreams. Then weaken me. Rid me of these dreams. Deliver me. Take whatever steps are required, so that I won't even have time enough to *dream* of being unfaithful to you. (And reality, in any case, is less absorbing.) But first make sure to brand me with your mark. If I sport the mark of your riding crop or your chains, or if I am still wearing those rings in my lips, let the whole world know I am yours. As long as I am beaten and ravished on your behalf, I am naught but the thought of you, the desire of you, the obsession of you. That, I believe, is what you wanted. Well, I love you, and that is what I want too.

"If I have ceased, once and for all, to be my own mistress, if my mouth and loins and breasts no longer belong to me, then I become a creature of another world, a world in which everything has a new meaning. Perhaps one day I shall have lost all knowledge about myself. Then what will pleasure matter to me, what will the caresses of so many men—your envoys, whom I am incapable of telling one from the other—mean to me, when I can no longer compare them to you?"

This is the way she speaks. I listen to her, and I can see that she isn't lying. I try to follow her (what bothered me for a long time was her prostitution). Perhaps, after all, the burning mantle of mythology is not a simple allegory, and sacred prostitution no mere historical curiosity. It may be that the chains in naive folk songs, and the "I would die for love of thee" are not mere metaphors, and that when streetwalkers tell their pimps: "I've got you under my skin; do whatever you like with me," this too is no simple figure of speech. (It is strange how, when we are intent upon ridding ourselves of some feeling which baffles us, we ascribe it to hoodlums and whores.) It may be that when Héloïse wrote to Abelard: "I shall be thy whore," she was not merely turning a pretty phrase. Without doubt, *Story of O* is the most ardent love letter any man has ever received.

I am reminded of the Dutchman who was fated to sail the seven seas as long as he failed to find a girl ready to give up her life to save him; and of the knight Guiguemar who, to be healed of his wounds, awaited a woman who would suffer for him "what no woman has ever suffered." To be sure, the story of O is longer than a lay or a legend, and far more detailed than a simple letter. Perhaps it also had to rise from greater depths. Perhaps it has never been more difficult than it is today to understand what boys and girls are saying in the streets—much the same thing, I suspect, that the Barbados slaves were saying. We live in a time when the simplest truths have no choice but to come back to us naked (like O), clothed in the mask of an owl.

For today we hear seemingly normal people, even those with a level head on their shoulders, blithely speaking of love as though it were some frothy feeling of no real consequence. They say it offers many pleasures, and that this contact of two epidermises is not completely devoid of charm. They go on to say that charm or pleasure is most rewarding for the person who is capable of keeping love imaginative, capricious, and above all natural and free. Far be it from me to object, and if it's all that simple for two people of the opposite sex (or even of the same sex) to give each other a good time, then indeed they should, they would be crazy not to. There are only one or two words in all this which disturb me: the word *love*, and also the word *free*. Needless to say, it is quite the opposite. Love implies dependence—not only in its pleasure but by its very existence and in what precedes its existence: in our very desire to exist—dependence on half a hundred odd little things: on two lips (and the smile or grimace they make), on a shoulder (and the special way it has of rising or falling), on two eyes (and their expression, a little more flirtatious or forbidding), or, when you come down to it, on the whole foreign body, with the mind and soul enclosed therein—a body which is capable at any moment of becoming more dazzling than the sun, more freezing than a tract of snowy waste. To undergo the experience is no fun, you make me laugh with your entreaties. When this body stoops down to fasten the buckle of her dainty shoe, you tremble, and you have the feeling the whole world is watching you. Rather the whip, the rings in the flesh! As for freedom . . . any man, or any woman, who has been through the experience will rather be inclined to rant and rave against freedom, in the vilest, most horrible language possible. No, there is no dearth of abominations in *Story of O*. But it sometimes seems to me that it is an idea, or a complex of ideas, an opinion rather than a young woman we see being subjected to these tortures.

The Truth about the Revolt

Strange, that the notion of happiness in slavery should today seem so novel. There is virtually nothing left of the ancient law which gives the family the power of life and death over their children; corporal punishment and hazing have practically been eliminated from the schools, and the old prerogative of wife-beating banished from the home. Men who in past centuries were proudly decapitated on public squares are now left cheerlessly to rot in dank cellars. The only tortures we inflict these days are undeserved and anonymous ones. Therefore, they are a thousand times more terrible, and wars today manage to roast, in a single, searing blast, the population of an entire city. The excessive kindness of father, teacher, or lover is paid for by blankets of napalm bombs and the atomic explosion. Everything happens as though there exists in the world a mysterious equilibrium of violence, for which we have lost all taste, and even our understanding of the term. And, personally, I am not displeased that it is a woman who has found them again. I am not even surprised.

To tell the truth, I do not have as many preconceived ideas about women as most men do. I am surprised there are any (women). More than surprised: somewhat amazed and filled with admiration. This perhaps explains why they seem so marvelous to me, and why I can't stop envying them. What is it precisely that I envy?

There are times when I regret my lost childhood. What I regret, though, are not the surprises and the revelations of which the poets speak. No. I remember a time when I thought I was responsible for the whole world. I was by turns a champion boxer or a cook, an orator-politician (yes), a general, a thief, even a redskin, a tree, or a rock. I shall be told that this was only a game. Yes, for you adults it may have been, but not for me, not in the least. This was when I bore the whole weight of the world on my shoulders, with all the cares and dangers it comprised: this is when I was universal. What I am trying to say is this:

Women at least are fated to resemble, throughout their lives, the children we once were. A woman understands a thousand things which totally escape me. She generally knows how to sew. She knows how to cook. She knows how to decorate an apartment and can tell which styles clash (I'm not saying she knows how to do all these things perfectly, but then I wasn't a perfect little redskin either). And she knows a lot more besides. She's comfortable with dogs and cats; she's able to converse with those half-mad creatures we allow among us, children: she teaches them cosmology and how to behave, to wash their hands and brush their teeth and other basics of hygiene, and she tells them fairy tales; and she has even been known to go so far as to teach them the piano. In short, from earliest childhood we are constantly dreaming of a man who would be all men at once. But it would appear that to each woman is given the capacity to be all women (and all men) at once. And there is something even more curious.

We hear it said nowadays that to understand fully is to forgive fully. Now, it has always seemed to me that with women—however universal they may be—it is just the opposite. I've had a fair number of friends who have always accepted me for what I am, and I in turn have taken them for what they are—without the slightest desire on my part or on theirs to change one another. I might even say that I was delighted—as were they—that each of us was so unique, so unlike the others. But there is not a woman alive who isn't interested in changing the man she loves, and at the same time changing herself. As though the proverb were lying, and the truth of the matter is that to understand fully is to forgive nothing at all.

No, Pauline Réage does not forgive very much. And I even wonder, to pursue this thought to its conclusion, whether she does not exaggerate slightly, whether her fellow-females, her peers, are actually as much alike as she assumes. But this is what more than one man is all too willing to grant her.

Should we regret the loss of the notebook compiled by the Barbados slaves? I fear, I must confess, that the worthy Anabaptist who drew it up may have cluttered it, in the section dedicated to apologetics, with a fair number of platitudes: for instance, that there will always be slaves, (which, in any case, seems to be borne out by the evidence); that they will always be the same (which is open to question); that one must resign oneself to one's condition and not waste in recriminations a time that might better be spent in games, meditation, and customary pleasures. And so on and so forth. But I suspect that he was not telling the truth, which is that Glenelg's slaves were in love with their master, that they could not bear to be without him. The same truth, after all, which lends *Story of O* its resolute quality, its incredible decency, and that strong, fanatic wind which never ceases to blow.

I

The Lovers of Roissy

*H*er lover one day takes O for a walk in a section of the city where they never go—the Montsouris Park, the Monceau Park. After they have taken a stroll in the park and have sat together side by side on the edge of a lawn, they notice, at one corner of the park, at an intersection where there are never any taxis, a car which, because of its meter, resembles a taxi.

"Get in," he says.

She gets in. It is autumn, and coming up to dusk. She is dressed as she always is: high heels, a suit with a pleated skirt, a silk blouse, and no hat. But long gloves which come up over the sleeves of her jacket, and in her leather handbag she has her identification papers, her compact, and her lipstick.

The taxi moves off slowly, the man still not having said a word to the driver. But he pulls down the shades of the windows on both sides of the car, and the shade on the back window. She has taken off her gloves, thinking he wants to kiss her or that he wants her to caress him. But instead he says:

"Your bag's in your way; let me have it."

3

She gives it to him. He puts it out of her reach and adds:

"You also have on too many clothes. Unfasten your stockings and roll them down to above your knees. Here are some garters."

By now the taxi has picked up speed, and she has some trouble managing it; she's also afraid the driver may turn around. Finally, though, the stockings are rolled down, and she's embarrassed to feel her legs naked and free beneath her silk slip. Besides, the loose garter-belt suspenders are slipping back and forth.

"Unfasten your garter belt," he says, "and take off your panties."

That's easy enough, all she has to do is slip her hands behind her back and raise herself slightly. He takes the garter belt and panties from her, opens her bag and puts them in, then says:

"You shouldn't sit on your slip and skirt. Pull them up behind you and sit directly on the seat."

The seat is made of some sort of imitation leather which is slippery and cold: it's quite an extraordinary sensation to feel it sticking to your thighs. Then he says:

"Now put your gloves back on."

The taxi is still moving along at a good clip, and she doesn't dare ask why René just sits there without moving or saying another word, nor can she guess what all this means to him—having her there motionless, silent, so stripped and exposed, so thoroughly gloved, in a black car going God knows where. He hasn't told her what to do or what not to do, but she's afraid either to cross her legs or press them together. She sits with gloved hands braced on either side of her seat.

"Here we are," he says suddenly. Here we are: the taxi stops on a lovely avenue, beneath a tree—they are plane trees—in front of some sort of small private home which can be seen nestled between the courtyard and the garden, the type of small private dwelling one finds along the Faubourg Saint-Germain. The street lamps are some distance away, and it is still fairly dark inside the car. Outside it is raining.

"Don't move," René says. "Sit perfectly still."

His hand reaches for the collar of her blouse, unties the bow, then unbuttons the blouse. She leans forward slightly, thinking he wants to fondle her breasts. No. He is merely groping for the shoulder straps of her brassiere, which he snips with a small penknife. Then he takes it off. Now, beneath her blouse, which he has buttoned back up, her breasts are naked and free, as is the rest of her body, from waist to knee.

"Listen," he says. "Now you're ready. This is where I leave you. You're to get out and go ring the doorbell. Follow whoever opens the door for you, and do whatever you're told. If you hesitate about going in, they'll come and take you in. If you don't obey immediately, they'll force you to. Your bag? No, you have no further need for your bag. You're merely the girl I'm furnishing. Yes, of course I'll be there. Now run along."

Another version of the same beginning was simpler and more direct: the young woman, dressed in the same way, was driven by her lover and an unknown friend. The stranger was driving, the lover was seated next to the young woman, and it was the unknown friend who explained to the young woman that her lover had been entrusted with the task of getting her ready, that he was going to tie her hands behind her back, unfasten her stockings and roll them down, remove her garter belt, her

5

panties, and her brassiere, and blindfold her. That she would then be turned over to the château, where in due course she would be instructed as to what she should do. And, in fact, as soon as she had been thus undressed and bound, they helped her to alight from the car after a trip that lasted half an hour, guided her up a few steps and, with her blindfold still on, through one or two doors. Then, when her blindfold was removed, she found herself standing alone in a dark room, where they left her for half an hour, or an hour, or two hours, I can't be sure, but it seemed forever. Then, when at last the door was opened and the light turned on, you could see that she had been waiting in a very conventional, comfortable, yet distinctive room: there was a thick rug on the floor, but not a stick of furniture, and all four walls were lined with closets. The door had been opened by two women, two young and beautiful women dressed in the garb of pretty eighteenth-century chambermaids: full skirts made out of some light material, which were long enough to conceal their feet; tight bodices, laced or hooked in front, which sharply accentuated the bust line; lace frills around the neck; half-length sleeves. They were wearing eye shadow and lipstick. Both wore a close-fitting collar and had tight bracelets on their wrists.

I know it was at this point that they freed O's hands, which were still tied behind her back, and told her to get undressed, they were going to bathe her and make her up. They proceeded to strip her till she hadn't a stitch of clothing left, then put her clothes away neatly in one of the closets. She was not allowed to bathe herself, and they did her hair as at the hairdresser's, making her sit in one of those large chairs which tilts back when they wash your hair and straightens back up after the hair has been set and you're ready for the dryer. That always takes at least an hour. Actually it took more than an hour, but she was seated on this chair, naked, and they kept her from either crossing her legs or bringing them together. And since the wall in front of her was covered from floor to ceiling with a large mirror, which was unbroken by any shelving, she could see herself, thus open, each time her gaze strayed to the mirror.

When she was properly made up and prepared—her eyelids penciled lightly; her lips bright red; the tip and halo of her breasts highlighted with pink; the edges of her nether lips rouged; her armpits and pubis generously perfumed, and perfume also applied to the furrow between her thighs, the furrow beneath her breasts, and to the hollows of her hands—she was led into a room where a three-sided mirror, and another mirror behind, enabled her to examine herself closely. She was told to sit down on the ottoman, which was set between the mirrors, and wait. The ottoman was covered with black fur, which pricked her slightly; the rug was black, the walls red. She was wearing red mules. Set in one of the walls of the small bedroom was a large window, which looked out onto a lovely, dark park. The rain had stopped, the trees were swaying in the wind, the moon raced high among the clouds.

I have no idea how long she remained in the red bedroom, or whether she was really alone, as she surmised, or whether someone was watching her through a peephole camouflaged in the wall. All I know is that when the two women returned, one was carrying a dressmaker's tape measure and the other a basket. With them came a man dressed in a long purple robe, the sleeves of which were gathered at the wrists and full at the shoulders. When he walked the robe flared open, from the waist down. One could see that beneath his robe he had on some sort of tights which covered his legs and thighs but left the sex exposed. It was the sex that O saw first, when he took his first step, then the whip, made of leather thongs, which he had stuck in his belt. Then she saw that the man was masked by a black hood—which concealed even his eyes behind a network of black gauze—and, finally, that he was also wearing fine black kid gloves.

Using the familiar *tu* form of address, he told her not to move and ordered the women to hurry. The woman with the tape then took the measurements of O's neck and wrists. Though on the small side, her measurements were in no way out of the ordinary, and it was easy enough to find the right-sized collar and bracelets, in the basket the other woman was carrying. Both collar and bracelets were made of several layers of leather (each layer being fairly thin, so that the total was no more than the thickness of a finger). They had clasps, which functioned automatically like a padlock when it closes, and they could be opened only by means of a small key. Imbedded in the layers of leather, directly opposite the lock, was a snugly-fitting metal ring, which allowed one to get a grip on the bracelet, if one wanted to attach it, for both collar and bracelets fit the arms and neck so snugly—although not so tight as to be the least painful—that it was impossible to slip any bond inside.

So they fastened the collar and bracelets to her neck and wrists, and the man told her to get up. He took her place on the fur ottoman, called her over till she was touching his knees, slipped his gloved hand between her thighs and over her breasts, and explained to her that she would be presented that same evening, after she had dined alone.

She did in fact dine by herself, still naked, in a sort of little cabin where an invisible hand passed the dishes to

8

her through a small window in the door. Finally, when dinner was over, the two women came for her. In the bedroom, they fastened the two bracelet rings together behind her back. They attached a long red cape to the ring of her collar and draped it over her shoulders. It covered her completely, but opened when she walked, since, with her hands behind her back, she had no way of keeping it closed. One woman preceded her, opening the doors, and the other followed, closing them behind her. They crossed a vestibule, two drawing rooms, and went into the library, where four men were having coffee. They were wearing the same long robes as the first, but no masks. And yet O did not have time to see their faces or ascertain whether her lover was among them (he was), for one of the men shone a light in her eyes and blinded her. Everyone remained stock still, the two women flanking her and the men in front, studying her. Then the light went out; the women left. But O was blindfolded again. Then they made her walk forward—she stumbled slightly as she went—until she felt that she was standing in front of the fire around which the four men were seated: she could feel the heat, and in the silence she could hear the quiet crackling of the burning logs. She was facing the fire. Two hands lifted her cape, two others—after having checked to see that her bracelets were attached—descended the length of her back and buttocks. The hands were not gloved, and one of them penetrated her in both places at once, so abruptly that she cried out. Someone laughed. Someone else said:

"Turn her around, so we can see the breasts and the belly."

They turned her around, and the heat of the fire was against her back. A hand seized one of her breasts, a mouth fastened on the tip of the other. But suddenly she

9

lost her balance and fell backward (supported by whose arms?), while they opened her legs and gently spread her lips. Hair grazed the insides of her thighs. She heard them saying that they would have to make her kneel down. This they did. She was extremely uncomfortable in this position, especially because they forbade her to bring her knees together and because her arms pinioned behind her forced her to lean forward. Then they let her rock back a bit, so that she was half-sitting on her heels, as nuns are wont to do.

"You've never tied her up?"

"No, never."

"And never whipped her?"

"No, never whipped her either. But as a matter of fact..."

It was her lover speaking.

"As a matter of fact," the other voice went on, "if you do tie her up from time to time, or whip her just a little, and she begins to like it, that's no good either. You have to get past the pleasure stage, until you reach the stage of tears."

Then they made O get up and were on the verge of untying her, probably in order to attach her to some pole or wall, when someone protested that he wanted to take her first, right there on the spot. So they made her kneel down again, this time with her bust on an ottoman, her hands still tied behind her, with her hips higher than her torso. Then one of the men, holding her with both his hands on her hips, plunged into her belly. He yielded to a second. The third wanted to force his way into the narrower passage and, driving hard, made her scream. When he let her go, sobbing and befouled by tears beneath her blindfold, she slipped to the floor, only to feel someone's knees against her face, and she realized that her mouth was not to be

10

spared. Finally they let her go, a captive clothed in tawdry finery, lying on her back in front of the fire. She could hear glasses being filled and the sound of the men drinking, and the scraping of chairs. They put some more wood on the fire. All of a sudden they removed her blindfold. The large room, the walls of which were lined with bookcases, was dimly lit by a single wall lamp and by the light of the fire, which was beginning to burn more brightly. Two of the men were standing and smoking. Another was seated, a riding crop on his knees, and the one leaning over her fondling her breast was her lover. All four of them had taken her, and she had not been able to distinguish him from the others.

They explained to her that this was how it would always be, as long as she was in the château, that she would see the faces of those who violated or tormented her, but never at night, and she would never know which ones had been responsible for the worst. The same would be true when she was whipped, except that they wanted her to see herself being whipped, and so this once she would not be blindfolded. They, on the other hand, would don their masks, and she would no longer be able to tell them apart.

Her lover had helped her to her feet, still wrapped in her red cape, made her sit down on the arm of an easy chair near the fire, so that she could hear what they had to tell her and see what they wanted to show her. Her hands were still behind her back. They showed her the riding crop, which was long, black, and delicate, made of thin bamboo encased in leather, the kind one sees in the windows of better riding equipment shops; the leather whip, which the first man she had seen had been carrying in his belt, was long and consisted of six lashes knotted at the end. There was a third whip of fairly thin cords, each with several knots at the end: the cords were quite stiff, as

11

though they had been soaked in water, which in fact they had, as O discovered, for they caressed her belly with them and nudged open her thighs, so that she could feel how stiff and damp the cords were against the tender, inner skin. Then there were the keys and the steel chains on the console table. Along one entire wall of the library, halfway between floor and ceiling, ran a gallery which was supported by two columns. A hook was imbedded in one of them, just high enough for a man standing on tiptoe, with his arms stretched above his head, to reach. They told O, whose lover had taken her in his arms, with one hand supporting her shoulders, and the other in the furrow of her loins, which burned so she could hardly bear it, they told her that her hands would be untied, but merely so that they could be fastened anew, a short while later, to the pole, using these same bracelets and one of the steel chains. They said that, with the exception of her hands, which would be held just above her head, she would thus be able to move and see the blows coming: that in principle she would be whipped only on the thighs and buttocks, in other words between her waist and knees, in the same region which had been prepared in the car that had brought her here, when she had been made to sit naked on the seat; but that in all likelihood one of the four men present would want to mark her thighs with the riding crop, which makes lovely long deep welts which last a long time. She would not have to endure all this at once; there would be ample time for her to scream, to struggle, and to cry. They would grant her some respite, but as soon as she had caught her breath they would start in again, judging the results not from her screams or tears but from the size and color of the welts they had raised. They remarked to her that this method of judging the effectiveness of the whip—besides being equitable—also made it pointless for the victims to exaggerate their suffering in an effort to arouse pity, and thus enabled them to resort to the same measures beyond the château walls, outdoors in the park—as was often done—or in any ordinary apartment or hotel room, assuming a gag was used (such as the one they produced and showed her there on the spot), for the gag stifles all screams and eliminates all but the most violent moans, while allowing tears to flow without restraint.

There was no question of using it that night. On the contrary, they wanted to hear her scream; and the sooner the better. The pride she mustered to resist and remain silent did not long endure: they even heard her beg them to untie her, to stop for a second, just for a second. So frantically did she writhe, trying to escape the bite of the lashes, that she turned almost completely around, on the near side of the pole, for the chain which held her was long and, although quite solid, was fairly slack. As a result, her belly and the front of her thighs were almost as marked as her backside. They made up their minds, after in fact having stopped for a moment, to begin again only after a rope had been attached first to her waist, then to the pole. Since they tied her tightly, to keep her waist snug to the pole, her torso was forced slightly to one side, and this in turn caused her buttocks to protrude in the opposite direction. From then on the blows landed on their target, unless aimed deliberately elsewhere. Given the way her lover had handed her over, had delivered her into this situation, O might have assumed that to beg him for mercy would have been the surest method for making him redouble his cruelty, so great was his pleasure in extracting, or having the others extract, from her this unquestionable proof of his power. And indeed he was the first to point out that the leather whip, the first they had used on her, left almost no marks (in contrast to the whip made of water-soaked cords, which marked almost upon contact, and the riding crop, which raised immediate welts), and thus allowed them to prolong the agony and follow their fancies in starting and stopping. He asked them to use only the leather whip.

Meanwhile, the man who liked women only for what they had in common with men, seduced by the available behind which was straining at the bonds knotted just below the waist, a behind made all the more enticing by its efforts to dodge the blows, called for an intermission in order to take advantage of it. He spread the two parts, which burned beneath his hands, and penetrated—not without some difficulty—remarking as he did that the passage would have to be rendered more easily accessible. They all agreed that this could, and would, be done.

When they untied the young woman, she staggered and almost fainted, draped in her red cape. Before returning her to the cell she was to occupy, they sat her down in an armchair near the fire and outlined for her the rules and regulations she was to follow during her stay in the château and later in her daily life after she had left it (which did not mean regaining her freedom, however). Then they rang. The two young women who had first received her came in, bearing the clothes she was to wear during her stay and tokens by which those who had been hosts at the château before her arrival and those who would be after she had left, might recognize her. Her outfit was similar to theirs: a long dress with a full skirt, worn over a sturdy whalebone bodice gathered tightly at the waist, and over a stiffly starched linen petticoat. The low-cut neck scarcely concealed the breasts which, raised by the constricting bodice, were only lightly veiled by the network of lace. The petticoat was white, as was the lace,

14

and the dress and bodice were a sea-green satin. When O was dressed and resettled in her chair beside the fire, her pallor accentuated by the color of the dress, the two young women, who had not uttered a word, prepared to leave. One of the four friends seized one of them as she passed, made a sign for the other to wait, and brought the girl he had stopped back toward O. He turned her around and, holding her by the waist with one hand, lifted her skirt with the other, in order to demonstrate to O, he said, the practical advantages of the costume and show how well designed it was. He added that all one needed to keep the skirts raised was a simple belt, which made everything that lay beneath readily available. In fact, they often had the girls go about in the château or the park either like this, or with their skirts tucked up in front, waist high. They had the young woman show O how she would have to keep her skirt: rolled up several turns (like a lock of hair rolled in a curler) and secured tightly by a belt, either directly in front, to expose the belly, or in the middle of the back, to leave the buttocks free. In either case, skirt and petticoat fell diagonally away in large, cascading folds of intermingled material. Like O, the young woman's backside bore fresh welts from the riding crop. She left the room.

Here is the speech they then delivered to O:

"You are here to serve your masters. During the day, you will perform whatever domestic duties are assigned you, such as sweeping, putting back the books, arranging flowers, or waiting on table. Nothing more difficult than that. But at the first word or sign from anyone you will drop whatever you are doing and ready yourself for what is really your one and only duty: to lend yourself. Your hands are not your own, nor are your breasts, nor, most especially, any of your bodily orifices, which we may explore or penetrate at will. You will remember at all times—or as constantly as possible—that you have lost all right to privacy or concealment, and as a reminder of this fact, in our presence you will never close your lips completely, or cross your legs, or press your knees together (you may recall you were forbidden to do this the minute you arrived). This will serve as a constant reminder, to you as well as to us, that your mouth, your belly, and your backside are open to us. You will never touch your breasts in our presence: the bodice raises them toward us, that they may be ours. During the day you will therefore be dressed, and if anyone should order you to lift your skirt, you will lift it; if anyone desires to use you in any manner whatsoever, he will use you, unmasked, but with this one reservation: the whip. The whip will be used only between dusk and dawn. But besides the whipping you receive from whoever may want to whip you, you will also be flogged in the evening, as punishment for any infractions of the rules committed during the day: for having been slow to oblige, for having raised your eyes and looked at the person addressing you or taking you—you must never look any of us in the face. If the costume we wear in the evening—the one I am now wearing—leaves our sex exposed, it is not for the sake of convenience, for it would be just as convenient the other way, but for the sake of insolence, so that your eyes will be directed there upon it and nowhere else, so that you may learn that there resides your master, for whom, above all else, your lips are intended. During the day, when we are dressed in normal attire and you are clothed as you are now, the same rules will apply, except that when requested you will open your clothes, and then close them again when we have finished with you. Another thing: at night you will have only your lips with which to honor us—and your

16

widespread thighs—for your hands will be tied behind your back and you will be naked, as you were a short while ago. You will be blindfolded only to be maltreated and, now that you have seen how you are whipped, to be flogged. And yes, by the way: while it is perfectly all right for you to grow accustomed to being whipped—since you are going to be every day throughout your stay—this is less for our pleasure than for your enlightenment. How true this is may be shown by the fact that on those nights when no one desires you, you will wait until the valet whose job it is comes to your solitary cell and administers what you are due to receive but we are not in the mood to mete out. Actually, both this flogging and the chain—which when attached to the ring of your collar keeps you more or less closely confined to your bed several hours a day—are intended less to make you suffer, scream, or shed tears than to make you feel, *through* this suffering, that you are not free but fettered, and to teach you that you are totally dedicated to something outside yourself. When you leave here, you will be wearing on your third finger an iron ring, which will identify you. By then you will have learned to obey those who wear the same insignia, and when they see it they will know that beneath your skirt you are constantly naked, however comely or commonplace your clothes may be, and that this nakedness is for them. Should anyone find you in the least intractable, he will return you here. Now you will be shown to your cell."

While they were talking to O, the two women who had come to dress her had been standing on either side of the stake where she had been whipped, without touching it, as though it terrified them, or as though they had been forbidden to touch it (which was more likely); when the man had finished, they came over to O, who realized that

17

she was supposed to get up and follow them. She therefore got up, gathering her skirts in her arms to keep from tripping, for she was not used to long dresses and did not feel steady on the mules with thick soles and very high heels which only a thick satin strap, of the same green as her dress, kept from slipping off her feet. As she bent down she turned her head. The women were waiting, the men were no longer looking at her. Her lover, seated on the floor leaning against the ottoman over which she had been thrown at the beginning of the evening, with his knees raised and his elbows on his knees, was toying with the leather whip. As she took her first step to join the women, her skirt grazed him. He raised his head and smiled, calling her by her name, and he too stood up. Softly he caressed her hair, smoothed her eyebrows with the tip of his finger, and softly kissed her on the lips. In a loud voice, he told her that he loved her. O, trembling, was terrified to notice that she answered "I love you," and that it was true. He pulled her against him and said: "Darling, sweetheart," kissed her on the neck and the curve of the cheek; she had let her head fall on his shoulder, which was covered by the purple robe. Very softly this time he repeated to her that he loved her, and very softly added: "You're going to kneel down, caress me, and kiss me," and he pushed her away, signaling to the women to move aside so he could lean back against the console. He was tall, but the table was not very high and his long legs, sheathed in the same purple as his robe, were bent. The open robe stiffened from beneath like drapes, and the top of the console table slightly raised his heavy sex and the light fleece above it. The three men approached. O knelt down on the rug, her green dress in a corolla around her. Her bodice squeezed her; her breasts, whose nipples were visible, were at the level of her lover's

18

knees. "A little more light," said one of the men. As they were adjusting the lamp so that the beam of light would fall directly on his sex and on his mistress's face, which was almost touching it, and on her hands which were caressing him from below, René suddenly ordered: "Say it again: I love you." O repeated "I love you," with such delight that her lips hardly dared brush the tip of his sex, which was still protected by its sheath of soft flesh. The three men, who were smoking, commented on her gestures, on the movement of her mouth closed and locked on the sex she had seized, as it worked its way up and down, on the way tears streamed down her ravaged face each time the swollen member struck the back of her throat and made her gag, depressing her tongue and causing her to feel nauseous. It was this same mouth which, half gagging on the hardened flesh which filled it, murmured again: "I love you." The two women had taken up positions to the right and left of René, who had one arm around each of their shoulders. O could hear the comments made by those present, but through their words she strained to hear her lover's moans, caressing him carefully, slowly, and with infinite respect, the way she knew pleased him. O felt that her mouth was beautiful, since her lover condescended to thrust himself into it, since he deigned publicly to offer caresses to it, since, finally, he deigned to discharge in it. She received it as a god is received, she heard him cry out, heard the others laugh, and when she had received it she fell, her face against the floor. The two women picked her up, and this time they led her away.

The mules banged on the red tiles of the hallway, where doors succeeded doors, discreet and clean, with tiny locks, like the doors of the rooms in big hotels. O was working up the courage to ask whether each of these rooms was occupied, and by whom, when one of her companions, whose voice she had not yet heard, said to her:

"You're in the red wing, and your valet's name is Pierre."

"What valet?" said O, struck by the gentleness of the voice. "And what's your name?"

"Andrée."

"Mine is Jeanne," said the second.

"The valet is the one who has the keys," the first one went on, "the one who will chain and unchain you, who will whip you when you are to be punished and when the others have no time for you."

"I was in the red wing last year," Jeanne said. "Pierre was there already. He often came in at night. The valets have the keys and the right to use any of us in the rooms of their section."

O was about to ask what kind of a person this Pierre was, but she did not have time to. As they turned a corner of the hallway, they made her halt before a door similar in all respects to the others: on a bench between this and the following door she noticed a sort of thick-set, ruddy peasant, whose head was practically clean shaved, with small black eyes set deep in his skull and rolls of flesh on his neck. He was dressed like the valet in some operetta: a shirt whose lace frills peeked out from beneath his black vest, which itself was covered by a red jacket of the kind called a spencer. He had black breeches, white stockings, and patent-leather pumps. He too was carrying a leather-thonged whip in his belt. His hands were covered with red hair. He took a master key from his vest pocket, opened the door, ushered the three women in, and said:

"I'm locking the door. Ring when you've finished."

20

The cell was quite small, and actually consisted of two rooms. With the hall door closed, they found themselves in an antechamber which opened into the cell proper; in this same wall, inside the room itself, was another door which opened into the bathroom. Opposite the doors there was the window. Against the left wall, between the doors and the window, stood the head of a large square bed, which was very low and covered with furs. There was no other furniture, no mirror. The walls were bright red, and the rug black. Andrée pointed out to O that the bed was less a bed than a mattressed platform covered with a black, long-haired imitation fur material. The pillow, hard and flat like the mattress, was of the same reversible material. The only object on any of the walls was a thick, gleaming steel ring which was set at about the same height above the bed as the hook in the stake had been above the floor of the library; from it descended a long steel chain directly onto the bed, its links forming a little pile, the other end being attached at arm's length to a padlocked hook, like a drapery pulled back and held in place by a curtain loop.

"We have to give you your bath," Jeanne said. "I'll unfasten your dress."

The only peculiar features of the bathroom were the Turkish-type toilet, located in the corner nearest the door, and the fact that every inch of wall space was covered with mirrors. Jeanne and Andrée did not allow O to go in until she was naked. They put her dress away in the closet next to the washbasin, where her mules and red cape already were, and remained with her, so that when she had to squat down over the porcelain pedestal she found herself surrounded by a whole host of reflections, as exposed as in the library when unknown hands had taken her by force.

"Wait until it's Pierre," said Jeanne, "and you'll see."

"Why Pierre?"

"When he comes to chain you, he may make you squat."

O felt herself turn pale. "But why?" she said.

"Because you have to," Jeanne replied. "But you're lucky."

"Why lucky?"

"Was it your lover who brought you here?"

"Yes," O said.

"They'll be a lot harder with you."

"I don't understand. . . ."

"You will very soon. I'm ringing for Pierre. We'll come and get you tomorrow morning."

Andrée smiled as she left and Jeanne, before following her, caressed the tips of O's breasts. O, completely taken aback, remained standing at the foot of the bed. With the exception of the collar and leather bracelets, which the water had stiffened when she had bathed and were tighter than before, O was naked.

"Behold the lovely lady," said the valet as he entered. And he seized both her hands. He slipped one of the bracelet hooks into the other, so that her wrists were tightly joined, then clipped both these hooks to the ring of the necklace. Thus her hands were joined as in an attitude of prayer, at the level of her neck. All that remained to be done was to chain her to the wall with the chain that was lying on the bed and was attached to the ring above. He unfastened the hook by which the other end was attached and pulled on it in order to shorten it. O was forced to move to the head of the bed, where he made her lie down. The chain clicked in the ring, and was so tight that the young woman could do no more than move from one side of the bed to the other or stand up on either side of the headboard. Since the chain tended to shorten the collar, that is, pull it backward, and her hands tended to pull it forward, an equilibrium was established, with her joined hands lying on her left shoulder and her head bending in that direction as well. The valet pulled the black cover up over O, but not before he had lifted her legs for a moment and pushed them back toward her chest, to examine the cleft between her thighs. He did not touch her further, did not say a word, turned out the light, which was a bracket lamp on the wall between the two doors, and went out.

Lying on her left side, alone in the darkness and silence, hot beneath her two layers of fur, of necessity motionless, O tried to figure out why there was so much sweetness mingled with the terror in her, or why her terror seemed itself so sweet. She realized that one of the things that most distressed her was the fact that she had been deprived of the use of her hands; not that her hands could have defended her (and did she really want to defend herself?), but had they been free they would at least have made the gesture, have made an attempt to repel the hands which seized her, the flesh which pierced her, to protect her loins from the whip. O's hands had been taken away from her; her body beneath the fur was inaccessible to her. How strange it was not to be able to touch one's own knees, or the hollow of one's own belly. The lips between her legs, her burning lips were forbidden her, and perhaps they were burning because she knew they were open to the first comer: to the valet Pierre, if he cared to enter. She was surprised that the whipping she had received had left her so untroubled, so calm, whereas the thought that she would probably never know which of the four men had twice taken her from behind, and whether it was the same man both times, and whether it had been her lover, quite distressed her. She turned over slightly on her stomach, recalling that her lover loved the furrow between her buttocks which, except for this evening (if it had been he), he had never penetrated. She hoped it had been he; would she ask him? Ah, never! Again she saw the hand which in the car had taken her garter belt and panties, and had stretched the garters so that she could roll her stockings down to above her knees. The memory was so vivid that she forgot her hands were bound and made the chain grate. And why, if she took the memory of the torture she had gone through so lightly, why did the very idea, the very word or sight of a whip make her heart beat wildly and her eyes close with terror? She did not stop to consider whether it was only terror; she was overwhelmed with panic: they would pull on her chain and haul her to her feet on the bed, and they would whip her, with her belly glued to the wall they would whip her, whip her, the word kept turning in her head. Pierre would whip her, Jeanne had said he would. You're lucky, Jeanne had repeated, they'll be a lot harder on you. What had she meant by that? She no longer felt anything but the collar, the bracelets, and the chain; her body was drifting away. She fell asleep.

In the wee hours of the night, just before dawn when it is darkest and coldest, Pierre reappeared. He turned on the light in the bathroom, leaving the door open so that a square of light fell on the middle of the bed, on the spot where O's slender body was curled, making a small mound beneath the cover, which silently he pulled back. Since O was sleeping on her left side, her face to the window and her legs slightly drawn up, the view she offered him was that of her white flanks, which seemed even whiter against the black fur. He took the pillow from beneath her head and said politely:

"Would you please stand up," and when she was on her knees, a position she managed by pulling herself up with the chain, he gave her a hand, taking her by the elbows so that she could stand up straight with her face to the wall. The square of light on the bed, which was faint, since the bed was black, illuminated her body, but not his gestures. She guessed, but could not see, that he was undoing the chain to rehook it to another link, so that it would remain taut, and she could feel it growing tighter. Her feet, which were bare, were solidly planted on the bed. Nor was she able to see that he had in his belt not the leather whip but the black riding crop similar to the one they had hit her with while she was tied to the stake, but they had only used it twice on her and had not hit her hard. She felt Pierre's left hand on her waist, the mattress gave a little as, to steady himself, he put his right foot on it. At the same time as she heard a whistling noise in the semi-darkness O felt a terrible burning across her back, and she screamed. Pierre flogged her with all his might. He did not wait for her screams to subside, but struck her again four times, being careful each time to lash her above or below the preceding spot, so that the traces would be all the clearer. Even after he had stopped she went on screaming, and the tears streamed down into her open mouth.

"Please be good enough to turn around," he said, and since she, who was completely distracted, failed to obey, he took her by the hips without letting go of his riding crop, the handle of which brushed against her waist. When she was facing him, he moved back slightly and lowered his crop on the front of her thighs as hard as he could. The whole thing had lasted five minutes. When he had left, after having turned out the light and closed the bathroom door, O was left moaning in the darkness, swaying back and forth along the wall at the end of her chain. She tried to stop moaning and to immobilize herself against the wall, whose gleaming percale was cool on her tortured flesh, as day slowly began to break. The tall window toward which she was turned, for she was leaning on one hip, was facing the east. It extended from floor to ceiling and, except for the drapes—of the same red material as that on the wall— which graced it on either side and split into stiff folds below the curtain loops which held it, had no curtains. O watched the slow birth of pale dawn, trailing its mist among the clusters of asters outside at the foot of her window, until finally a poplar tree appeared. The yellow leaves from time to time fell in swirls, although there was no wind. In front of the window, beyond the bed of purple asters, there was a lawn, at the end of which was a pathway. It was broad daylight by now, and O had not moved for a long time. A gardener appeared on the path, pushing a wheelbarrow. The iron wheel could be heard squeaking over the gravel. If he had come over to rake the leaves that had fallen in among the asters, the window was so tall and the room so small and bright that he would have seen O chained and naked, and the marks of the riding crop on her thighs. The cuts were swollen, and had formed narrow swellings much darker in color than the red of the walls. Where was her lover sleeping, the way he loved to sleep on quiet mornings? In what room, in what bed? Was he aware of the pain, the tortures to which he had delivered her? Was he the one who had decided what they would be? O recalled the prisoners she had seen in engravings and in history books, who also had been chained and whipped many years ago, centuries ago, and had died. She did not wish to die, but if torture was the

26

price she had to pay to keep her lover's love, then she only hoped he was pleased that she had endured it. All soft and silent she waited, waited for them to bring her back to him.

None of the women had the keys to any locks, neither the locks to the doors nor the chains, the collars or bracelets, but every man carried a ring of three sets of keys, each of which, in the various categories, opened all the doors or all the padlocks, or all the collars. The valets had them too. But in the morning the valets who had been on the night shift were sleeping, and it was one of the masters or another valet who came to open the locks. The man who came into O's cell was dressed in a leather jacket and was wearing riding breeches and boots. She did not recognize him. First he unlocked the chain on the wall, and O was able to lie down on the bed. Before he unlocked her wrists, he ran his hand between her thighs, the way the first man with mask and gloves, whom she had seen in the small red drawing room, had done. It may have been the same one. His face was bony and fleshless, with that piercing look one associates with the portraits of old Huguenots, and his hair was gray. O met his gaze for what seemed to be an endless time and, suddenly freezing, she remembered it was forbidden to look at the masters above the belt. She closed her eyes, but it was too late, and she heard him laugh and say, as he finally freed her hands:

"There will be a punishment for that after dinner."

He said something to Jeanne and Andrée, who had come in with him and were standing waiting on either side of the bed, after which he left. Andrée picked up the pillow which was on the floor, and the blanket that Pierre had turned down toward the foot of the bed when he had come to whip O, while Jeanne wheeled, toward the head of the bed, a serving table which had been brought into the hallway and on which were coffee, milk, sugar, bread, croissants, and butter.

"Hurry up and eat," said Andrée. "It's nine o'clock. Afterward you can sleep till noon, and when you hear the bell it will be time to get ready for lunch. You'll bathe and fix your hair. I'll come to make you up and lace up your bodice."

"You won't be on duty till afternoon," Jeanne said. "In the library: you'll serve the coffee and liqueur and tend the fire."

"And what about you?" O said.

"We're only supposed to take care of you during the first twenty-four hours of your stay. After that you're on your own, and will have dealings only with the men. We won't be able to talk to you, and you won't be able to talk to us either."

"Don't go," O said. "Stay a while longer and tell me . . ." But she did not have time to finish her sentence. The door opened: it was her lover, and he was not alone. It was her lover, dressed the way he used to when he had just gotten out of bed and lighted the first cigarette of the day: in striped pajamas and a blue dressing gown, the wool robe with the padded silk lapels which they had picked out together a year before. And his slippers were worn, she would have to buy him another pair. The two women disappeared, with no other sound except the rustling of silk as they lifted their skirts (all the skirts were a trifle long and trailed on the ground)—on the carpet the mules could not be heard.

O, who was holding a cup of coffee in her left hand and a croissant in the other, was seated cross-legged, or rather half-cross-legged, on the edge of the bed, one of her legs dangling and the other tucked up under her. She did not move, but her cup suddenly began to shake in her hand, and she dropped the croissant.

"Pick it up," René said. They were his first words.

She put the cup down on the table, picked up the partly eaten croissant, and put it beside the cup. A fat croissant crumb still lay on the rug, beside her bare foot. This time René bent down and picked it up. Then he sat down near O, pulled her back down onto the bed, and kissed her. She asked him if he loved her. He answered: "Yes, I love you!" then got to his feet and made her stand up too, softly running the cool palms of his hands, then his lips, over the welts.

Since he had come in with her lover, O did not know whether or not she could look at the man who had entered with him and who, for the moment, had his back to them and was smoking a cigarette near the door. What followed was not of a nature to reassure her.

"Come over here so we can see you," her lover said, and having guided her to the foot of the bed, he pointed out to his companion that he had been right, and he thanked him, adding that it would only be fair for him to take O first if he so desired.

The unknown man, whom she still did not dare to look at, then asked her, after having run his hand over her breasts and down her buttocks, to spread her legs.

"Do as he says," said René, who was holding her up. He too was standing, and her back was against him. With his right hand he was caressing one breast, and his other was on her shoulder. The unknown man had sat down on the edge of the bed, he had seized and slowly parted, drawing the fleece, the lips which protected the entrance itself. René pushed her forward, as soon as he realized what was wanted from her, so that she would be more

29

accessible, and his right arm slipped around her waist, giving him a better grip.

This caress, to which she never submitted without a struggle and which always filled her with shame, and from which she escaped as quickly as she could, so quickly in fact that she had scarcely had a chance to be touched, this caress which seemed a sacrilege to her, for she deemed it sacrilege for her lover to be on his knees, feeling that she should be on hers, she suddenly felt that she would not escape from it now, and she saw herself doomed. For she moaned when the alien lips, which were pressing upon the mound of flesh whence the inner corolla emanates, suddenly inflamed her, left her to allow the hot tip of the tongue to inflame her even more; she moaned even more when the lips began again: she felt the hidden point harden and rise, that point caught in a long, sucking bite between teeth and lips, which did not let go, a long, soothing bite which made her gasp for breath. She lost her footing and found herself again lying on the bed, with René's mouth on her mouth; his two hands were pinning her shoulders to the bed, while two other hands beneath her knees were raising and opening her legs. Her own hands, which were beneath her back (for when René had propelled her toward the unknown man he had bound her wrists together by clipping the wristbands together), were grazed by the sex of the man who was caressing himself in the furrow of her buttocks before rising to strike hard into the depths of her belly. At the first stroke she cried out, as though it had been the lash of a whip, then again at each new stroke, and her lover bit her mouth. The man tore himself abruptly away from her and fell back on the floor, as though struck by lightning, and he too gave a cry.

René freed O's hands, lifted her up, and lay her down

beneath the blanket on the bed. The man got up, René escorted him to the door. In a flash, O saw herself released, reduced to nothing, accursed. She had moaned beneath the lips of the stranger as never her lover had made her moan, cried out under the impact of a stranger's member as never her lover had made her cry out. She felt debased and guilty. She could not blame him if he were to leave her. But no, the door was closing again, he was staying with her, he was coming back, lying down beside her beneath the cover, he was slipping into her moist, hot belly and, still holding her in this embrace, he said to her:

"I love you. When I'll also have given you to the valets, I'll come in one night and have you flogged till you bleed."

The sun had broken through the mist and flooded the room. But only the midday bell woke them up.

O was at a loss what to do. Her lover was there, as close, as tenderly relaxed and surrendered as he was in the bed in that low-ceilinged room to which, almost every night since they had begun living together, he came to sleep with her. It was a big, mahogany, English-style four-poster bed, without the awning, and the posters at the head were taller than those at the foot. He always slept on her left, and whenever he awoke, even were it in the middle of the night, his hands inevitably reached down for her legs. This is why she never wore anything but a nightgown or, if she had on pajamas, never put on the bottoms. He did so now; she took that hand and kissed it, without ever daring to ask him for anything. But he spoke. Holding her by the collar, with two fingers slipped in between the neck and collar, he told her it was his intention that henceforth she should be shared by him and those of his choosing, and by those whom he did not know who were connected

31

to the society of the château, shared as she had been the previous evening. That she was dependent on him, and on him alone, even though she might receive orders from persons other than himself, whether he was present or absent, for as a matter of principle he was participating in whatever might be demanded of or inflicted on her, and that it was he who possessed and enjoyed her through those into whose hands she had been given, by the simple fact that he had given her to them. She must greet them and submit to them with the same respect with which she greeted him, as though they were so many reflections of him. Thus he would possess her as a god possesses his creatures, whom he lays hold of in the guise of a monster or a bird, of an invisible spirit or a state of ecstasy. He did not wish to leave her. The more he surrendered her, the more he would hold her dear. The fact that he gave her was to him a proof, and ought to be one for her as well, that she belonged to him: one can only give what belongs to you. He gave her only to reclaim her immediately, to reclaim her enriched in his eyes, like some common object which had been used for some divine purpose and has thus been consecrated. For a long time he had wanted to prostitute her, and he was delighted to feel that the pleasure he was deriving was even greater than he had hoped, and that it bound him to her all the more, as it bound her to him, all the more so because, through it, she would be more humiliated and ravaged. Since she loved him, she could not help loving whatever derived from him. O listened and trembled with happiness, because he loved her, all acquiescent she trembled. He doubtless guessed it, for he went on:

"It's because it's easy for you to consent that I want from you what it will be impossible for you to consent to, even if you agree ahead of time, even if you say yes now and imagine yourself capable of submitting. You won't be able *not* to revolt. Your submission will be obtained in spite of you, not only for the inimitable pleasure that I and others will derive from it, but also so that you will be made aware of what has been done to you."

O was on the verge of saying that she was his slave and that she bore her bonds cheerfully. He stopped her.

"Yesterday you were told that as long as you are in the château you are not to look a man in the face or speak to him. The same applies to me as well: with me you shall remain silent and obey. I love you. Now get up. From now on the only times you will open your mouth here in the presence of a man will be to cry out or to caress."

So O got up. René remained lying on the bed. She bathed and arranged her hair. The contact of her bruised loins with the tepid water made her shiver, and she had to sponge herself without rubbing to keep from reviving the burning pain. She made up her mouth but not her eyes, powdered herself and, still naked but with lowered eyes, came back into the room.

René was looking at Jeanne, who had come in and was standing at the head of the bed, she too with her head bowed, unspeaking. He told her to dress O. Jeanne took the bodice of green satin, the white petticoat, the dress, the green mules and, having hooked up O's bodice in front, began to lace it up tight in the back. The bodice was long and stiff, stoutly whaleboned as during the period when wasp waists were in style, with gussets to support the breasts. The more the bodice was tightened, the more the breasts were lifted, supported as they were by the gussets, and the nipples displayed more prominently. At the same time, the constriction of the waist caused her stomach to protrude and her backside to arch out sharply. The strange thing was that this armor was very comfortable and to a certain extent restful. It made you stand up very straight, but it made you realize—why, it was hard to tell unless it was by contrast—the freedom, or rather the availability, of that part of the body left unrestricted. The full skirt and the trapezoid-shaped neckline running from the base of the neck to the tips of the breasts and across the full length of the bosom, seemed to the girl to be less a protective outfit than an instrument designed to provoke or present. When Jeanne had tied the laces in a double knot, O took her dress from the bed. It was a one-piece dress, with the petticoat attached to the skirt like a detachable lining, and the bodice, cross-laced in front and tied in the back, was thus able to follow more or less the delicate contours of her bosom, depending on how tightly the bodice was laced. Jeanne had laced it very tight, and through the open door O was able to see herself reflected in the bathroom mirror, slim and lost in the green satin which billowed at her hips, as a hoop skirt would have done. The two women were standing side by side. Jeanne reached out to smooth a wrinkle in the green dress, and her breasts stirred in the lace fringes of her bodice, breasts whose tips were long and the halos brown. Her dress was of yellow faille.

René, who had come over to the two women, said to O: "Watch." And to Jeanne: "Lift your dress." With both hands she raised the crackling silk and the crinoline which lined it, revealing as she did a golden belly, gleaming thighs and knees, and a tight black triangle. René put his hand on it and slowly explored, and with the other excited the nipple of one breast.

"Merely so you can see," he said to O.

O saw. She saw his ironic but attentive face, his eyes carefully watching Jeanne's half-open mouth and her neck, which was thrown back, tightly circled by the leather collar. What pleasure was she giving him, yes she, that this girl or any other could not?

"That hadn't occurred to you?" he added.

No, that had not occurred to her. She had collapsed against the wall, between the two doors, her arms hanging limp. There was no longer any need to tell her to keep quiet. How could she have spoken? Perhaps he was touched by her despair. He left Jeanne and took her in his arms, calling her his love and his life, saying over and over again that he loved her. The hand he was caressing her neck with was moist with the odor of Jeanne. And so? The despair which had overwhelmed her slowly ebbed: he loved her, ah he loved her. He was free to enjoy himself with Jeanne, or with others, he loved her. "I love you," he had whispered in her ear, "I love you," so softly it was scarcely audible. "I love you." He did not leave until he saw that her eyes were clear and her expression calm, contented.

Jeanne took O by the hand and led her out into the hallway. Their mules again made a resounding noise on the tile floor, and again they found a valet seated on a bench between the doors. He was dressed like Pierre, but it was not Pierre. This one was tall, dry, and had dark hair. He preceded them and showed them into an antechamber where, before a wrought-iron door which stood between two tall green drapes, two other valets were waiting, some white dogs with russet spots lying at their feet.

"That's the enclosure," Jeanne murmured. But the valet who was walking in front of them heard her and turned around. O was amazed to see Jeanne turn deathly pale and let go of her hand, let go of her dress which she was holding lightly with her other hand, and sink to her knees on the black tile floor—for the antechamber was tiled in black marble. The two valets near the gate burst out laughing. One of them came over to O and politely invited her to follow him, opened a door opposite the one she had just entered, and stood aside. She heard laughter and the sound of footsteps, then the door closed behind her. She never—no, never—learned what had happened, whether Jeanne had been punished for having spoken, and if so what the punishment had been, or whether she had simply yielded to a caprice on the part of the valet, or whether in throwing herself on her knees she had been obeying some rule or trying to move the valet to pity, and whether she had succeeded. During her initial stay in the château, which lasted two weeks, she only noted that, although the rule of silence was absolute, it was rare that they did not try and break it while they were alone with the valets, either being taken to or from some place in the château, or during meals, especially during the day. It was as though clothing gave them a feeling of assurance which nakedness and nocturnal chains, and the masters' presence, destroyed. She also noticed that, whereas the slightest gesture which might have been construed as an advance toward one of the masters seemed quite naturally inconceivable, the same was not true for the valets. They never gave orders, although the courtesy of their requests was as implacable as an order. They had apparently been enjoined to punish to the letter infractions of the rules which occurred in their presence, and to punish them on the spot. Thus on three occasions O saw girls who were caught talking thrown to the floor and whipped—once in the hallway leading to the red wing, and twice again in the refectory they had just entered. So it was possible to be whipped in broad daylight, despite what they had told her

36

the first evening, as though what happened with the valets did not count and was left to their discretion.

Daylight made their outfits look strange and menacing. Some valets wore black stockings and, in place of the red jacket and the white ruffled shirt, a soft, wide-sleeved shirt of red silk, gathered at the neck and with the sleeves also gathered at the wrists. It was one of these valets who, on the eighth day at noon, his whip already in his hand, made a buxom blonde named Madeleine, who was seated not far from O, get up off her stool. Madeleine, whose bosom was all milk and roses, had smiled at him and spoken a few words so quickly that O had missed them. Before he had time to touch her she was on her knees, her hands, so white against the black silk, lightly stroking the still dormant sex, which she took out and brought to her half-open mouth. That time she was not whipped. And since he was then the only monitor in the refectory, and since he closed his eyes as he accepted the caress, the other girls began talking. So it was possible to bribe the valets. But what was the use? If there was one rule to which O had trouble submitting, and indeed never really submitted to completely, it was the rule forbidding them to look the men in the face—considering that the rule applied to the valets as well, O felt herself in constant danger, so compelling was her curiosity about faces, and she was in fact whipped by both the valets, not, in truth, each time they noticed her doing it (for they took some liberties with the instructions, and perhaps cared enough about the fascination they exercised not to deprive themselves, by too strict or efficacious an application of the rules, of the gazes which would leave their face or mouth only to return to their sex, their whips, and their hands, and then start in all over again), but only when in all probability they wanted to humiliate her. No matter how

37

cruelly they treated her when they had made up their minds to do so, she none the less never had the courage, or the cowardice, to throw herself at their knees, and though she submitted to them at times she never tempted or urged them on. As for the rule of silence, it meant so little to her that, except in the case of her lover, she did not once break it, replying by signals whenever another girl would take advantage of their guards' momentary distraction to speak to her. This was generally during meals, which were taken in the room into which they had been ushered, when the tall valet accompanying them had turned around to Jeanne. The walls were black and the stone floor was black, the long table, of heavy glass, was black too, and each girl had a round stool covered with black leather on which to sit. They had to lift their skirts to sit down, and in so doing O rediscovered, the moment she felt the smooth, cold leather beneath her thighs, that first moment when her lover had made her take off her stockings and panties and sit in the same manner on the back seat of the car. Conversely, after she had left the château and, dressed like everyone else except for the fact that beneath her innocuous suit or dress she was naked, whenever she had to lift her petticoat and skirt to sit down beside her lover, or beside another, were it on the seat of a car or the bench of a café, it was the château she rediscovered, the breasts proffered in the silk bodices, the hands and mouths to which nothing was denied, and the terrible silence. And yet nothing had been such a comfort to her as the silence, unless it was the chains. The chains and the silence, which should have bound her deep within herself, which should have smothered her, strangled her, on the contrary freed her from herself. What would have become of her if she had been granted the right to speak and the freedom of her hands, if she had been free to make a choice, when her lover prostituted her before his own eyes? True, she did speak as she was being tortured, but can moans and cries be classed as words? Besides, they often stilled her by gagging. Beneath the gazes, beneath the hands, beneath the sexes that defiled her, the whips that rent her, she lost herself in a delirious absence from herself which restored her to love and, perhaps, brought her to the edge of death. She was anyone, anyone at all, any one of the other girls, opened and forced like her, girls whom she saw being opened and forced, for she did see it, even when she was not obliged to have a hand in it.

Thus, less than twenty-four hours after her arrival, during her second day there, she was taken after the meal into the library, there to serve coffee and tend the fire. Jeanne, whom the black-haired valet had brought back, went with her as did another girl named Monique. It was this same valet who took them there and remained in the room, stationed near the stake to which O had been attached. The library was still empty. The French doors faced west, and in the vast, almost cloudless sky the autumn sun slowly pursued its course, its rays lighting, on a chest of drawers, an enormous bouquet of sulphur-colored chrysanthemums which smelled of earth and dead leaves.

"Did Pierre mark you last night?" the valet asked O.

She nodded that he had.

"Then you should show it," he said. "Please roll up your dress."

He waited till she had rolled her robe up behind, the way Jeanne had done the evening before, and till Jeanne had helped her fasten it there. Then he told her to light the fire. O's backside up to her waist, her thighs, her slender legs, were framed in the cascading folds of green silk and white linen. The five welts had turned black. The fire was ready on the hearth, all O had to do was ignite the straw beneath the kindling, which leaped into flame. Soon the branches of apple wood caught, then the oak logs, which burned with tall, crackling, almost colorless flames which were almost invisible in the daylight, but which smelled good. Another valet entered and placed a tray filled with coffee cups on the console, from which the lamp had been removed, then left the room. O went over near the console, while Monique and Jeanne remained standing on either side of the fireplace.

Just then two men came in, and the first valet in turn left the room. O thought she recognized one of the men from his voice, one of those who had forced her the previous evening, the one who had asked that her rear be made more easily accessible. As she poured the coffee into the small black and gold cups, which Monique handed around with the sugar, she stole a glance at them. So it was this thin, blond boy, a mere stripling, with an English air about him. He was speaking again; now she was certain. The other man was also fair, thick set with a heavy face. Both of them were seated in the big leather armchairs, their feet near the fire, quietly smoking and reading their papers, paying no more heed to the women than if they had not been there. Now and then the rustle of a paper was heard, or the sound of coals falling on the hearth. From time to time O put another log on the fire. She was seated on a cushion on the floor beside the wood basket, Monique and Jeanne, also on the floor, across from her. Their flowing skirts overlapped one another. Monique's skirt was a dark red. Suddenly, but only after an hour had elapsed, the blond boy called Jeanne, then Monique. He told them to bring the ottoman (it was the same ottoman on which O had been spread-eagled the night before). Monique did not wait for further instructions, she kneeled down, bent over, her breasts crushed against the fur and holding both corners of the ottoman in her hands. When the young man had Jeanne lift the red skirt, she did not stir. Jeanne was then obliged to undo his clothing—and he gave her the order in the most churlish manner—and take between her hands that sword of flesh which had so cruelly pierced O at least once. It swelled and stiffened beneath the closed palm, and O saw these same hands, Jeanne's tiny hands, spreading Monique's thighs, into the hollow of which, slowly and in short spasms which made her moan, the lad plunged.

The other man, who was watching in silence, motioned to O to approach and, without taking his eyes off the spectacle, toppled her forward over one arm of his chair—and her raised skirt gave him an unhindered view of her backside—and seized her womb with his hand.

It was in this position that René found her when, a minute later, he opened the door.

"Please don't let me disturb you," he said, and he sat down on the floor, on the same cushion where O had been sitting beside the fire before she had been called. He watched her closely, and smiled every time the hand which was holding her probed and returned, seizing both front and rear apertures at once and working deeper and deeper as they opened further, wrenching from her a moan which she could no longer restrain.

Monique had long since gotten back to her feet, Jeanne was fiddling with the fire in place of O. She brought René a glass of whisky, and he kissed her hand as she handed it to him, then drank it down without taking his eyes off O.

The man who was still holding her then said:

"Is she yours?"

"Yes," René replied.

41

"James is right," the other went on, "she's too narrow. She has to be widened."

"Not too much, mind you," said James.

"Whatever you say," René said, getting to his feet. "You're a better judge than I." And he rang.

For the next eight days, between dusk when her stint in the library came to an end and that hour of the night—which was generally eight or ten o'clock—when she was returned to her cell, in chains and naked beneath her red cape, O wore an ebonite shaft simulating an erect male member which was inserted behind and held in place by three small chains connected to a leather belt around her hips, in such a way that the internal movements of her muscles could not expel it. One little chain followed the furrow of her buttocks, the two others the fold on either side of the belly's triangle, in order not to prevent anyone from penetrating that side if need be.

When René had rung, it was to have the coffer brought in which contained, or one of whose compartments contained, an assortment of small chains and belts, and whose other held a variety of these shafts, ranging from the very thin to the very thick. They all had one feature in common, namely that they flared at the base, to make it impossible for them to slide up inside the body, an accident which might have produced the opposite effect from that desired, that is it might have allowed the ring of flesh to tighten up again, whereas the purpose of the shaft was to distend it. Thus quartered, and quartered each day a little more, for James, who made her kneel down, or rather lie prone, to watch while Jeanne or Monique, or whichever girl happened to be there, fastened the shaft that he had chosen, each day chose a thicker one. At the evening meal, which the girls took together in the same refectory, after their bath, naked and powdered, O still wore it, and everyone could see that she was wearing it, because of the little chains and the belt. It was only removed, by the valet, when he came to chain her to the wall for the night if no one had asked for her, or, if someone had, when he locked her hands behind her if he had to take her to the library. Rare were the nights when someone did not appear to make use of this passage thus rapidly rendered as easy as, though still narrower than, the other. After eight days, there was no longer any need for an instrument, and O's lover told her that he was happy she was now doubly open and that he would make certain she remained so. At the same time, he warned her that he was leaving and that she would not see him during the last seven days she was to spend in the château, before he came back to pick her up and take her back to Paris.

"But I love you," he added, "I do love you. Don't forget me."

Oh, how could she forget him! He was the hand that blindfolded her, the whip wielded by the valet Pierre, he was the chain above her head, the unknown man who came down on her, and all the voices which gave her orders were his voice. Was she growing weary? No. By dint of being defiled and desecrated, it seems that she must have grown used to outrages, by dint of being caressed, to caresses, if not to the whip by dint of being whipped. A terrible surfeit of pain and pleasure should have by slow degrees cast her upon benumbing banks, into a state bordering on sleep or somnambulism. On the contrary. The bodice which held her straight, the chains which kept her submissive, her refuge of silence—these may have been responsible in part—as was the constant spectacle of girls being handed over and used as she was and, even when they were not, the spectacle of the

43

constantly available bodies. Also the spectacle and the awareness of her own body. Daily and, so to speak, ceremoniously soiled with saliva and sperm, she felt herself literally to be the repository of impurity, the sink mentioned in the Scriptures. And yet those parts of her body most constantly offended, having become less sensitive, at the same time seemed to her to have become more beautiful and, as it were, ennobled: her mouth closed upon anonymous members, the tips of her breasts constantly fondled by hands, and between her quartered thighs the twin, contiguous paths wantonly ploughed. That she should have been ennobled and gained in dignity through being prostituted was a source of surprise, and yet dignity was indeed the right term. She was illuminated by it, as though from within, and her bearing bespoke calm, while on her face could be detected the serenity and imperceptible smile that one surmises rather than actually sees in the eyes of hermits.

When René had informed her that he was leaving, night had already fallen. O was naked in her cell, and was waiting for them to come and take her to the refectory. As for her lover, he was dressed as usual, in a suit he wore every day in town. When he took her in his arms, the rough tweed of his clothes irritated the tips of her breasts. He kissed her, lay her down on the bed, lay down beside her and, tenderly and slowly and gently, took her, alternating between the two tracks open to him, before finally spilling himself into her mouth, which he then kissed again.

"Before I leave," he said, "I would like to have you whipped, and this time I'll ask your permission. Do you agree?"

She agreed to it.

"I love you," he repeated. "Ring for Pierre."

She rang. Pierre chained her hands above her head, to the chain of the bed. When she was thus bound, her lover kissed her again, standing beside her on the bed. Again he told her that he loved her, then he got down off the bed and nodded for Pierre. He watched her struggle, so fruitlessly; he listened to her moans swell and become cries. When her tears flowed, he sent Pierre away. She still found the strength to tell him again that she loved him. Then he kissed her drenched face, her gasping mouth, undid her bonds, laid her down, and left.

To say that O began to await her lover the minute he left her is a vast understatement: she was henceforth nothing but vigil and night. During the day she was like a painted countenance, whose skin is soft and mouth is meek and—this was the only time that she abided by the rule—whose eyes were constantly lowered. She made and tended the fire, poured and offered the coffee and liqueurs, lighted the cigarettes, she arranged the flowers and folded the newspapers like a young girl in her parents' living room, so limpid with her open neck and leather collar, her tight bodice and prisoner's bracelets, that all it took for the men whom she was serving was to order her to remain by their sides while they were violating another girl to make them want to violate her as well; which doubtless explains why she was treated even worse than before. Had she sinned? or had her lover left her so that the very people to whom he had loaned her would feel freer to dispose of her? In any case, the fact remains that on the second day following his departure as, at nightfall, she had just undressed and was looking in the bathroom mirror at the almost vanished welts made by Pierre's riding crop on the front of her thighs, Pierre entered.

There were still two hours before dinner. He told her that she would not dine in the common room and said to get ready, pointing to the Turkish toilet in the corner, over which she had to squat, as Jeanne had warned her she would in the presence of Pierre. All the while she remained there, he stood contemplating her, she could see him in the mirrors, and see herself, and was incapable of holding back the water which escaped from her body. He waited then until she had bathed and powdered herself. She was going to get her mules and red cape when he stopped her and added, fastening her hands behind her back, that there was no need to, but that she should wait a moment for him. She sat down on a corner of the bed. Outside it was storming, a tempest of cold rain and wind, and the poplar tree near the window swayed back and forth beneath the gusts. From time to time a pale wet leaf would splatter against the windowpanes. It was as dark as in the middle of the night, although the hour of seven had not yet struck, for autumn was well advanced and the days were growing shorter.

When Pierre returned, he was carrying the same blindfold with which he had blindfolded her the first evening. He also had a long chain, which made a clanking noise, a chain similar to the one fastened to the wall. O had the impression that he couldn't make up his mind whether to put the blindfold or the chain on her first. She was gazing out at the rain, not caring what they wanted from her, thinking only that René had said he would come back, that there were still five days and five nights to go, and that she had no idea where he was or whether he was alone and, if he was not alone, who he was with. But he would come back. Pierre had laid the chain on the bed and, without interrupting O's daydream, had covered her eyes with the blindfold of black velvet. It was slightly rounded below the sockets of the eyes, and fitted the cheekbones perfectly, making it impossible to get the slightest peek or even to raise the eyelids. Blessèd darkness like unto her own night, never had O greeted it with such joy, blessèd chains that bore her away from herself.

Pierre fastened the chain to the ring in her collar and invited her to follow him. She got up, felt herself being pulled forward, and walked. Her bare feet were icy cold on the tiles, and she gathered she was following the hallway of the red wing; then the ground, which was still as cold, became rough underfoot: she was walking on a stone floor, made of sandstone or granite. Twice the valet made her stop, she heard the sound of a key in a lock, of a lock being turned and opened, then locked again. "Careful of the steps," said Pierre, and she went down a staircase, and once she stumbled. Pierre caught her around the waist. He had never touched her except to chain or beat her, but here he was now forcing her down onto the cold steps, which she tried to grasp with her bound hands to keep from slipping, and he was taking her breasts. His mouth moved from one to the other, and as he pressed against her, she could feel him slowly rising. He did not help her up until he had taken his pleasure with her. Damp and trembling with cold, she finally descended the last steps and heard another door open, which she went through and immediately felt a thick rug beneath her feet. There was another slight tug on the chain, then Pierre's hands were loosing her hands and untying her blindfold: she was in a round, vaulted room, which was very small and low: the walls and arches were of unplastered stone, and the joints in the masonry were visible. The chain which was attached to her collar was fastened to the wall by an eye-bolt opposite the door, which was set about three feet above the floor and allowed her to move no more than two steps forward. There was neither a bed nor anything that might have served as a bed, nor was there any blanket, only three or four Moroccan-type cushions, but they were out of reach and clearly not intended for her. Within reach, however, in a niche from which emanated the little light which lighted the room, was a wooden tray on which were some water, fruit, and bread. The heat from the radiators, which had been installed along the base of the walls and set into the walls themselves to form around the entire room a sort of burning plinth, was none the less insufficient to overcome the odor of earth and mud which is the odor of ancient prisons and, in old châteaux, of uninhabited dungeons. In that hot semi-darkness, into which no sound intruded, O soon lost all track of time. There was no longer any day or night, the light never went out. Pierre, or some other valet—it hardly mattered which—replaced the water, fruit, and bread on the tray whenever it was gone, and took her to bathe in a nearby dungeon. She never saw the men who came in, for each time a valet preceded them to blindfold her eyes, and removed it only after they had left. She also lost track of them, of who they were and how many there were, and neither her soft hands nor her lips blindly caressing were ever able to identify who they were touching. At times there were several, more often only one, but each time, before they came near her, she was made to kneel down facing the wall, the ring of her collar fastened to the same eye-bolt to which the chain was attached, and whipped. She placed her palms against the wall and pressed her face against the back of her hands, to keep from scratching it against the stones; but she scraped her knees and her breasts on them. Thus she lost track of the tortures and screams which were smothered by the vault. She waited. Suddenly time no longer

48

stood still. In her velvet night her chain was unfastened. She had been waiting for three months, three days, or ten days, or ten years. She felt herself being wrapped in a heavy cloth, and someone taking her by the shoulders and knees, lifting and carrying her. She found herself in her cell, lying under the black fur cover, it was early afternoon, her eyes were open, her hands free, and Rene was sitting beside her, stroking her hair.

"You must get dressed now," he said, "we're leaving."

She took a last bath, he brushed her hair, handed her powder and lipstick to her. When she returned to her cell, her suit, her blouse, her slip, her stockings, and her shoes were on the foot of the bed, as were her gloves and handbag. There was even the coat she wore over her suit when the weather turned brisk, and a square silk scarf to protect her neck, but no garter belt or panties. She dressed slowly, rolling her stockings down to just above her knees, and she did not put on her suitcoat because it was very warm in her cell. Just then, the man who had explained on the first evening what would be expected of her, came in. He unlocked the collar and bracelets which had held her captive for two weeks. Was she freed of them? or did she have the feeling something was missing? She said nothing, scarcely daring to run her hands over her wrists, not daring to lift them to her throat.

Then he asked her to choose, from among the exactly identical rings which he showed to her in a small wooden box, the one which fit her left ring finger. They were strange iron rings, banded with gold inside, and the signet was wide and as massive as that of an actual signet ring, but it was convex, and for design bore a three-spoked wheel inlaid in gold, with each spoke spiraling back upon itself like the solar wheel of the Celts. The second ring she tried, though a trifle snug, fit her exactly. It was heavy

49

on her hand, and the gold gleamed as though furtively in the dull gray of the polished iron. Why iron, and why gold, and this insignia she did not understand? It was impossible to talk in this room draped in red, where the chain was still on the wall above the bed, where the black, still rumpled cover was lying on the floor, this room into which the valet Pierre might emerge, was sure to emerge, absurd in his opera outfit, in the dull light of November.

She was wrong, Pierre did not appear. René had her put on the coat to her suit, and her long gloves which covered the bottom of her sleeves. She took her scarf, her bag, and carried her coat over her arm. The heels of her shoes made less noise on the hallway floor than had her mules, the doors were closed, the antechamber was empty. O was holding her lover by the hand. The stranger who was accompanying them opened the wrought-iron gates which Jeanne had said were the enclosure, which was now no longer guarded either by valets or dogs. He lifted one of the green velvet curtains and ushered them both through. The curtains fell back into place. They heard the gate closing. They were alone in another antechamber which looked onto the lawn. All there was left to do was descend the steps leading down from the stoop, before which O recognized the car.

She sat down next to her lover, who took the wheel and started off. After they had left the grounds, through the porte-cochère which was wide open, he stopped a few hundred meters farther on and kissed her. It was on the outskirts of a small, peaceful town, which they crossed through as they continued on their route. O was able to read the name on the road sign: Roissy.

II

Sir Stephen

*T*he apartment where O lived was situated on the Ile
Saint-Louis, under the eaves of an old house which
faced south and overlooked the Seine. All the rooms,
which were spacious and low, had sloping ceilings, and
the two rooms at the front of the house each opened onto
a balcony set into the sloping roof. One of them was O's
room; the other, in which bookshelves filled one wall from
floor to ceiling on either side of the fireplace, served as a
living room, a study, and even as a bedroom in case of
necessity. Facing the two windows was a big couch, and
there was a large antique table before the fireplace. It
was here that they dined whenever the tiny dining room,
which faced the interior courtyard and was decorated
with dark green serge, was really too small to accommo-
date the guests. Another room, which also looked onto
the courtyard, was René's, and it was here that he dressed
and kept his clothes. O shared the yellow bathroom with
him; the kitchen, also yellow, was tiny. A cleaning woman
came in every day. The flooring of the rooms overlooking
the courtyard was of red tile, those antique hexagonal
tiles which in old Paris hotels are used to cover the stairs
and landings above the second story. Seeing them again

53

gave O a shock and made her heart beat faster: they were the same tiles as the ones in the hallways at Roissy. Her room was small, the pink and black chintz curtains were closed, the fire was glowing behind the metallic screen, the bed was made, the covers turned back.

"I bought you a nylon nightgown," René said. "You've never had one before."

Yes, a white pleated nylon nightgown, tailored and tasteful like the clothing of Egyptian statuettes, an almost transparent nightgown was unfolded on the edge of the bed, on the side where O slept. O tied a thin belt around her waist, over the elastic waistband of the nightgown itself, and the material of the gown was so light that the projection of the buttocks colored it a pale pink. Everything—save for the curtains and the panel hung with the same material against which the head of the bed was set, and the two small armchairs upholstered with the same chintz—everything in the room was white: the walls, the fringe around the mahogany four-poster bed, and the bearskin rug on the floor. Seated before the fire in her white nightgown, O listened to her lover.

He began by saying that she should not think that she was now free. With one exception, and that was that she was free not to love him any longer, and to leave him immediately. But if she did love him, then she was in no wise free. She listened to him without saying a word, thinking how happy she was that he wanted to prove to himself—it mattered little how—that she belonged to him, and thinking too that he was more than a little naive not to realize that this proprietorship was beyond any proof. But did he perhaps realize it and want to emphasize it merely because he derived a certain pleasure from it? She gazed into the fire as he talked, but he did not, not daring to meet her eyes. He was standing, pacing back and forth.

Suddenly he said to her that, for a start, he wanted her to listen to him with her knees unclasped and her arms unfolded, for she was sitting with her knees together and her arms folded around them. So she lifted her nightgown and, on her knees, or, rather, squatting on her heels in the manner of Carmelites or of Japanese women, she waited. The only thing was, since her knees were spread, she could feel the light, sharp pricking of the white fur between her half-open thighs; he came back to it again: she was not opening her legs wide enough. The word "open" and the expression "opening her legs" were, on her lover's lips, charged with such uneasiness and power that she could never hear them without experiencing a kind of internal prostration, a sacred submission, as though a god, and not he, had spoken to her. So she remained motionless, and her hands were lying palm upward beside her knees, between which the material of her nightgown was spread, with the pleats reforming.

What her lover wanted from her was very simple: that she be constantly and immediately accessible. It was not enough for him to know that she was: she was to be so without the slightest obstacle intervening, and her bearing and clothing both were to bespeak, as it were, the symbol of that availability to experienced eyes. That, he went on, meant two things. The first she knew, having been informed of it the evening of her arrival at the château: that she must never cross her knees, as her lips had always to remain open. She doubtless thought that this was nothing (that was indeed what she did think), but she would learn that to maintain this discipline would require a constant effort on her part, an effort which would remind her, in the secret they shared between them and perhaps with a few others, of the reality of her condition, when she was with those who did not share the secret, and engaged in ordinary pursuits.

As for her clothes, it was up to her to choose them, or if need be to invent them, so that this semi-undressing to which he had subjected her in the car on their way to Roissy would no longer be necessary: tomorrow she was to go through her closet and sort out her dresses, and to do the same with her underclothing by going through her dresser drawers. She would hand over to him absolutely everything she found in the way of belts and panties; the same for any brassieres like the one whose straps he had had to cut before he could remove it, any full slips which covered her breasts, all the blouses and dresses which did not open up the front, and any skirts too tight to be raised with a single movement. She was to have other brassieres, other blouses, other dresses made. Meanwhile, was she supposed to visit her corset maker with nothing on under her blouse or sweater? Yes, she was to go with nothing on underneath. If someone should notice, she could explain it any way she liked, or not explain it at all, whichever she preferred, but it was her problem, and hers alone. Now, as for the rest of what he still had to teach her, he preferred to wait for a few days and wanted her to be dressed properly before hearing it. She would find all the money she needed in the little drawer of her desk. When he had finished speaking, she murmured "I love you" without the slightest gesture. It was he who added some wood to the fire, lighted the bedside lamp, which was of pink opaline. Then he told O to get into bed and wait for him, that he would sleep with her. When he came back, O reached over to turn out the lamp: it was her left hand, and the last thing she saw before the room was plunged into darkness was the somber glitter of her iron ring. She was lying half on her side: her lover called her softly by name and,

56

simultaneously, seizing her with his whole hand, covered the nether part of her belly and drew her to him.

The next day, O, in her dressing gown, had just finished lunch alone in the green dining room—René had left early in the morning and was not due home until evening, to take her out to dinner—when the phone rang. The phone was in the bedroom, beneath the lamp at the head of the bed. O sat down on the floor to answer it. It was René, who wanted to know whether the cleaning woman had left. Yes, she had just left, after having served lunch, and would not be back till the following morning.

"Have you started to sort out your clothes yet?" René said.

"I was just going to start," she answered, "but I got up late, took a bath, and it was noon before I was ready."

"Are you dressed?"

"No, I have on my nightgown and my dressing gown."

"Put the phone down, take off your robe and your nightgown."

O obeyed, so startled that the phone slipped from the bed where she had placed it down onto the white rug, and she thought she had been cut off. No, she had not been cut off.

"Are you naked?" René went on.

"Yes," she said. "But where are you calling from?"

He ignored her question, merely adding:

"Did you keep your ring on?"

She had kept her ring on.

Then he told her to remain as she was until he came home and to prepare, thus undressed, the suitcase of clothing she was to get rid of. Then he hung up.

It was past one o'clock, and the weather was lovely. A

small pool of sunlight fell on the rug, lighting the white nightgown and the corduroy dressing gown, pale green like the shells of fresh almonds, which O had let slip to the floor when she had taken them off. She picked them up and went to take them into the bathroom, to hang them up in a closet. On her way, she suddenly saw her reflection in one of the mirrors fastened to a door and which, together with another mirror covering part of the wall and a third on another door, formed a large three-faced mirror: all she was wearing was a pair of leather mules the same green as her dressing gown—and only slightly darker than the mules she wore at Roissy—and her ring. She was no longer wearing either a collar or leather bracelets, and she was alone, her own sole spectator. And yet never had she felt herself more totally committed to a will which was not her own, more totally a slave, and more content to be so.

When she bent down to open a drawer, she saw her breasts stir gently. It took her almost two hours to lay out on her bed the clothes which she then had to pack away in the suitcase. There was no problem about the panties; she made a little pile of them near one of the bedposts. The same for her brassieres, not one would stay, for they all had a strap in the back and fastened on the side. And yet she saw how she could have the same model made, by shifting the catch to the front, in the middle, directly beneath the cleavage of the breasts. The girdles and garter belts posed no further problems, but she hesitated to add to the pile the corset of pink satin brocade which laced up in the back and so closely resembled the bodice she had worn at Roissy. She put it aside on the dresser. That would be René's decision. He would also decide about the sweaters, all of which went on over the head and were tight at the neck, therefore could not be opened. But they

58

could be pulled up from the waist and thus bare the breasts. All the slips, however, were piled on her bed. In the dresser drawer there still remained a half-length slip of black faille, hemmed with a pleated flounce and fine Valenciennes lace, which was made to be worn under a pleated sun skirt of black wool which was too sheer not to be transparent. She would need other half-length slips, short, light-colored ones. She also realized that she would either have to give up wearing sheath dresses or else pick out the kind of dress that buttoned all the way down the front, in which case she would also have to have her slips made in such a way that they would open together with the dress. As for the petticoats, that was easy, the dresses too, but what would her dressmaker say about the under-clothes? She would explain that she wanted a detachable lining because she was cold-blooded. As a matter of fact, she was sensitive to the cold, and suddenly she wondered how in the world she would stand the winter cold when she was dressed so lightly?

When she had finally finished, and had kept from her entire wardrobe only her blouses, all of which buttoned down the front, her black pleated skirt, her coats of course, and the suit she had worn home from Roissy, she went to prepare tea. She turned up the thermostat in the kitchen; the cleaning woman had not filled the wood basket for the living-room fire, and O knew that her lover liked to find her in the living room beside the fire when he arrived home in the evening. She filled the basket from the wood-pile in the hallway closet, carried it back to the living-room fireplace, and lighted the fire. Thus she waited for him, curled up in a big easy chair, the tea tray beside her, waited for him to come home, but this time she waited, the way he had ordered her to, naked.

The first difficulty O encountered was in her work. Difficulty is perhaps an exaggeration. Astonishment would be a better term. O worked in the fashion department of a photography agency. This meant that it was she who photographed, in the studios where they had to pose for hours on end, the most exotic and prettiest girls whom the fashion designers had chosen to model their creations.

They were surprised that O had postponed her vacation until this late in the fall and had thus been away at a time of year when the fashion world was busiest, when the new collections were about to be presented. But that was nothing. What surprised them most was how changed she was. At first glance, they found it hard to say exactly what was changed about her, but none the less they felt it, and the more they observed her the more convinced they were. She stood and walked straighter, her eyes were clearer, but what was especially striking was her perfection when she was in repose, and how measured her gestures were.

She had always been a conservative dresser, the way girls do whose work resembles that of men, but she was so skillful that she brought it off; and because the other girls—who constituted her subjects—were constantly concerned, both professionally and personally, with clothing and its adornments, they were quick to note what might have passed unperceived to eyes other than theirs. Sweaters worn right next to the skin, which gently molded the contours of the breasts—René had finally consented to the sweaters—pleated skirts so prone to swirling when she turned: O wore them so often it was a little as though they formed a discreet uniform.

"Very little-girl-like," one of the models said to her one day, a blond, green-eyed model with high Slavic cheekbones and the olive complexion that goes with it. "But you shouldn't wear garters," she added. "You're going to ruin your legs."

This remark was occasioned by O, who, without stopping to think, had sat down somewhat hastily in her presence, and obliquely in front of her, on the arm of a big leather easy chair, and in so doing had lifted her skirt. The tall girl had glimpsed a flash of naked thigh above the rolled stocking, which covered the knee but stopped just above it.

O had seen her smile, so strangely that she wondered what the girl had been thinking at the time, or perhaps what she had understood. She adjusted her stockings, one at a time, pulling them up to tighten them, for it was not as easy to keep them tight this way as it was when the stockings ended at mid-thigh and were fastened to a garter belt, and answered Jacqueline, as though to justify herself:

"It's practical."

"Practical for what?" Jacqueline wanted to know.

"I dislike garter belts," O replied.

But Jacqueline was not listening to her and was looking at the iron ring.

During the next few days, O took some fifty photographs of Jacqueline. They were like nothing she had ever taken before. Never, perhaps, had she had such a model. Anyway, never before had she been able to extract such meaning and emotion from a face or body. And yet all she was aiming for was to make the silks, the furs, and the laces more beautiful by that sudden beauty of an elfin creature surprised by her reflection in the mirror, which Jacqueline became in the simplest blouse, as she did in the most elegant mink. She had short, thick, blond hair, only slightly curly, and at the least excuse she would cock her head slightly toward her left shoulder and nestle her cheek against the upturned collar of her fur, if she were wearing fur. O caught her once in this position, tender and smiling, her hair gently blown as though by a soft wind, and her smooth, hard cheekbone snuggled against the gray mink, soft and gray as the freshly fallen ashes of a wood fire. Her lips were slightly parted, and her eyes half-closed. Beneath the gleaming, liquid gloss of the photograph she looked like some blissful girl who had drowned, she was pale, so pale. O had had the picture printed with as little contrast as possible. She had taken another picture of Jacqueline which she found even more stunning: back lighted, it portrayed her bare-shouldered, with her delicate head, and her face as well, enveloped in a large-meshed black veil surmounted by an absurd double aigrette whose impalpable tufts crowned her like wisps of smoke; she was wearing an enormous robe of heavy brocaded silk, red like the dress of a bride in the Middle Ages, which came down to below her ankles, flared at the hips and tight at the waist, and the armature of which traced the outline of her bosom. It was what the dress designers called a gala gown, the kind no one ever wears. The spike-heeled sandals were also of red silk. And all the time Jacqueline was before O dressed in that gown and sandals, and that veil which was like the premonition of a mask, O, in her mind's eye, was completing, was innerly modifying the model: a trifle here, a trifle there— the waist drawn in a little tighter, the breasts slightly raised—and it was the same dress as at Roissy, the same dress that Jeanne had worn, the same smooth, heavy, cascading silk which one takes by the handful and raises whenever one is told to. . . . Why yes, Jacqueline was lifting it in just that way as she descended from the platform on which she had been posing for the past fifteen minutes. It was the same rustling, the same crackling of dried leaves. No one wears these gala gowns any longer? But they do. Jacqueline was also wearing a gold choker around her neck, and on her wrists two gold bracelets. O caught herself thinking that she would be more beautiful with a leather collar and leather bracelets. And then she did something she had never done before: she followed Jacqueline into the large dressing room adjacent to the studio, where the models dressed and made up and where they left their clothing and make-up kits after hours. She remained standing, leaning against the doorjamb, her eyes glued to the mirror of the dressing table before which Jacqueline, without removing her gown, had sat down. The mirror was so big—it covered the entire back wall, and the dressing table itself was a simple slab of black glass—that she could see Jacqueline's and her own reflection, as well as the reflection of the costume girl who was undoing the aigrettes and the tulle netting. Jacqueline removed the choker herself, her bare arms lifted like two handles; a touch of perspiration gleamed in her armpits, which were shaved (Why? O wondered, what a pity, she's so fair), and O could smell the sharp, delicate, slightly plantlike odor and wondered what perfume Jacqueline ought to wear—what perfume they would make her wear. Then Jacqueline unclasped her bracelets and put them on the glass slab, where they made a momentary clanking sound like the sound of chains. Her hair was so fair that her skin was actually darker than her hair, a grayish beige like fine-grained sand just after the tide has gone out. On the photograph, the red silk would be black. Just then, the thick eyelashes, which Jacqueline was always reluctant to make up, lifted, and in the mirror O met her gaze, a look so direct and steady that, without being able to detach her own eyes from it, she felt herself slowly blushing. That was all.

"I'm sorry," Jacqueline said, "I have to undress."

"Sorry," O murmured, and closed the door.

The next day she took home with her the proofs of the shots she had made the day before, not really knowing whether she wanted, or did not want, to show them to her lover, with whom she had a dinner date. She looked at them as she was putting on her make-up at the dressing table in her room, pausing to trace on the photographs with her finger the curve of an eyebrow, the suggestion of a smile. But when she heard the sound of the key in the front door, she slipped them into the drawer.

For two weeks, O had been completely outfitted and ready for use, and could not get used to being so, when she discovered one evening upon returning from the studio a note from her lover asking her to be ready at eight to join him and one of his friends for dinner. A car would stop by to pick her up, the chauffeur would come up and ring her bell. The postscript specified that she was to take her fur jacket, that she was to dress entirely in black (*entirely* was underlined), and was to be at pains to make up and perfume herself as at Roissy.

It was six o'clock. Entirely in black, and for dinner—and it was mid-December, the weather was cold, that meant black silk stockings, black gloves, her pleated fan-shaped skirt, a heavy-knit sweater with spangles or her short jacket of faille. She decided on the jacket of faille. It was padded and quilted in large stitches, close fitting and hooked from neck to waist like the tight-fitting doublets that men used to wear in the sixteenth century, and if it molded the bosom so perfectly, it was because the brassiere was built into it. It was lined of the same faille, and its slit tails were hip length. The only bright foil were the large gold hooks like those on children's snow boots which made a clicking sound as they were hooked or unhooked from their broad flat rings.

After she had laid out her clothes on her bed, and at the foot of the bed her black suede shoes with raised soles and spiked heels, nothing seemed stranger to O than to see herself, solitary and free in her bathroom, meticulously making herself up and perfuming herself, after she had taken her bath, as she had done at Roissy. The cosmetics she owned were not the same as those used at Roissy. In the drawer of her dressing table she found some face rouge—she never used any—which she utilized to emphasize the halo of her breasts. It was a rouge which was scarcely visible when first applied, but which darkened later. At first she thought she had put on too much and tried to take a little off with alcohol—it was very hard to remove—and started all over: a dark peony pink flowered at the tips of her breasts. Vainly she tried to make up the lips which the fleece of her loins concealed, but the rouge left no mark. Finally, among the tubes of lipstick she had in the same drawer, she found one of those kissproof lipsticks which she did not like to use because they were too dry and too hard to remove. There, it worked. She fixed her hair and freshened her face, then finally put on the perfume. René had given her, in an atomizer which released a heavy spray, a perfume whose name she didn't know, which had the odor of dry wood and marshy plants, a pungent, slightly savage odor. On her skin the spray melted, on the fur of the armpits and belly it ran and formed tiny droplets.

At Roissy O had learned to take her time: she perfumed herself three times, each time allowing the perfume to dry. First she put on her stockings and high heels, then the petticoat and skirt, then the jacket. She put on her gloves and took her bag. In her bag were her compact, her lipstick, a comb, her key, and ten francs. Wearing her gloves, she took her fur coat from the closet and glanced at the time at the head of her bed: quarter to eight. She sat down diagonally on the edge of the bed and, her eyes riveted to the alarm clock, waited without moving for the bell to ring. When she heard it at last and rose to leave, she noticed in the mirror above her dressing table, before turning out the light, her bold, gentle, docile expression.

When she pushed open the door of the little Italian restaurant before which the car had stopped, the first person she saw, at the bar, was René. He smiled at her tenderly, took her by the hand, and turning toward a sort of grizzled athlete, introduced her in English to Sir Stephen H. O was offered a stool between the two men, and as she was about to sit down René said to her in a half-whisper to be careful not to muss her dress. He helped her to slide her skirt out from under her and down over the edges of the stool, the cold leather of which she felt against her skin, while the metal rim around it pressed directly against the furrow of her thighs, for at first she had dared only half sit down, for fear that if she were to sit down completely she might yield to the temptation to cross her legs. Her skirt billowed around her. Her right heel was caught in one of the rungs of the stool, the tip of her left foot was touching the floor. The Englishman, who had bowed without uttering a word, had not taken his eyes off her, she saw that he was looking at her knees, her hands, and finally at her lips—but so calmly and with such precise attention, with such self-assurance, that O felt herself being weighed and measured as the instrument she knew full well she was, and it was as though compelled by his gaze and, so to speak, in spite of herself that she withdrew her gloves: she knew that he would speak when her hands were bare—because she had unusual hands, more like those of a young boy than the hands of a woman, and because she was wearing on the third finger of her left hand the iron ring with the triple spiral of gold. But no, he said nothing, he smiled: he had seen the ring.

René was drinking a martini, Sir Stephen a whisky. He nursed his whisky, then waited till René had drunk his second martini and O the grapefruit juice that René had ordered for her, meanwhile explaining that if O would be good enough to concur in their joint opinion, they would dine in the room downstairs, which was smaller and less noisy than the one on the first floor, which was simply the extension of the bar.

"Of course," O said, already gathering up her bag and gloves which she had placed on the bar.

Then, to help her off the stool, Sir Stephen offered her his right hand, in which she placed hers, he finally addressing her directly by observing that she had hands that were made to wear irons, so becoming was iron to her. But as he said it in English, there was a trace of ambiguity in his words, leaving one in some doubt as to whether he was referring to the metal alone or whether he were not also, and perhaps even specifically, referring to iron chains.

In the room downstairs, which was a simple white-washed cellar, but cool and pleasant, there were in fact only four tables, one of which was occupied by guests who were finishing their meal. On the walls had been drawn, like a fresco, a gastronomical and tourist map of Italy, in soft, ice-cream colors: vanilla, raspberry, and pistachio. It reminded O that she wanted to order ice cream for dessert, with lots of almonds and whipped cream. For she was feeling light and happy, René's knee was touching her knee beneath the table, and whenever he spoke she knew he was talking for her ears alone. He too was observing her lips. They let her have the ice cream, but not the coffee. Sir Stephen invited O and René to have coffee at his place. They had all dined very lightly, and O realized that they had been careful to drink very little, and had kept her virtually from drinking at all: half a liter of Chianti for the three of them. They had also dined very quickly: it was barely nine o'clock.

"I sent the chauffeur home," said Sir Stephen. "Would you drive, René. The simplest thing would be to go straight to my house."

René took the wheel, O sat beside him, and Sir Stephen was next to her. The car was a big Buick, there was ample room for three people in the front seat.

After the Alma intersection, the Cours la Reine was visible because the trees were bare, and the Place de la Concorde sparkling and dry with, above it, the sort of sky which promises snow, but from which snow has not yet fallen. O heard a little click and felt the warm air rising around her legs: Sir Stephen had turned on the heater. René was still keeping to the Right Bank of the Seine, then he turned at the Pont Royal to cross over to the Left Bank: between its stone yokes, the water looked as frozen as the stone, and just as black. O thought of hematites, which are black. When she was fifteen her best friend, who was then thirty and with whom she was in love, wore a hematite ring set in a cluster of tiny diamonds. O would have liked a necklace of those black stones, without diamonds, a tight-fitting necklace, perhaps even a choker. But the necklaces that were given to her now—no, they were not given to her—would she exchange them for the necklace of hematites, for the hematites of the dream? She saw again the wretched room where Marion had taken her, behind the Turbigo intersection, and remembered how she had untied—she, not Marion—her two big schoolgirl pigtails when Marion had undressed her and laid her down on the iron bed. How lovely Marion was when she was being caressed, and it's true that eyes can resemble stars; hers looked like quivering blue stars.

René stopped the car. O did not recognize the little street, one of the cross streets which joins the rue de l'Université and the rue de Lille.

Sir Stephen's apartment was situated at the far end of a courtyard, in one wing of an old private mansion, and the rooms were laid out in a straight line, one opening into the next. The room at the very end was also the largest, and the most reposing, furnished in dark English mahogany and pale yellow and gray silk drapes.

"I shan't ask you to tend the fire," Sir Stephen said to O, "but this sofa is for you. Please sit down, René will make coffee. I would be most grateful if you would hear what I have to say."

The large sofa of light-colored Damascus silk was set at right angles to the fireplace, facing the windows which overlooked the garden and with its back to those behind, which looked onto the courtyard. O took off her fur and lay it over the back of the sofa. When she turned around, she noticed that her lover and her host were standing, waiting for her to accept Sir Stephen's invitation. She set her bag down next to her fur and unbuttoned her gloves. When, when would she ever learn, and would she ever learn, a gesture stealthy enough so that when she lifted her skirt no one would notice, so that she herself could forget her nakedness, her submission? Not, in any case, as long as René and that stranger were staring at her in silence, as they were presently doing. Finally she gave in. Sir Stephen stirred the fire, René suddenly went behind the sofa and, seizing O by the throat and the hair, pulled her head down against the back of the couch and kissed her on the mouth, a kiss so prolonged and profound that she gasped for breath and could feel her loins melting and burning. He let her go only long enough to tell her that he loved her, and then immediately took her again. O's hands, overturned in a gesture of utter abandon and defeat, her palms upward, lay quietly on her black dress that spread like a corolla around her. Sir Stephen had come nearer, and when at last René let her go and she opened her eyes, it was the gray, unflinching gaze of the Englishman which she encountered.

Completely stunned and bewildered, as she still was, and gasping with joy, she none the less was easily able to see that he was admiring her, and that he desired her. Who could have resisted her moist, half-open mouth, with its full lips, the white stalk of her arching neck against the black collar of her page-boy jacket, her eyes large and clear, which refused to be evasive? But the only gesture Sir Stephen allowed himself was to run his finger softly over her eyebrows, then over her lips. Then he sat down facing her on the opposite side of the fireplace, and when René had also sat down in an armchair, he began to speak.

"I don't believe René has ever spoken to you about his family," he said. "Still, perhaps you do know that his mother, before she married his father, had previously been married to an Englishman, who had a son from his first marriage. I am that son, and it was she who raised me, until she left my father. So René and I are not actually relatives, and yet, in a way, we are brothers. That René loves you I have no doubt. I would have known even if he hadn't told me, even if he hadn't made a move: all one has to do is to see the way he looks at you. I know too that you are among those girls who have been to Roissy, and I imagine you'll be going back again. In principle, the ring you're wearing gives me the right to do with you what I will, as it does to all those men who know its meaning. But that involves merely a fleeting assignation, and what we expect from you is more serious. I say 'we' because, as you see, René is saying nothing: he prefers to have me speak for both of us.

"If we are brothers, I am the eldest, ten years older than he. There is also between us a freedom so absolute and of such long standing that what belongs to me has always belonged to him, and what belongs to him has likewise belonged to me. Will you agree to join with us? I beg of you to, and I ask you to swear to it because it will involve more than your submission, which I know we can count on. Before you reply, realize for a moment that I am only, and can only be, another form of your lover: you will still have only one master. A more formidable one, I grant you, than the men to whom you were surrendered at Roissy, because I shall be there every day, and besides I am fond of habits and rites. . . ." (This last phrase he uttered in English.)

Sir Stephen's quiet, self-assured voice rose in an absolute silence. Even the flames in the fireplace flickered noiselessly. O was frozen to the sofa like a butterfly impaled upon a pin, a long pin composed of words and looks which pierced the middle of her body and pressed her naked, attentive loins against the warm silk. She was no longer mistress of her breasts, her hands, the nape of her neck. But of this much she was sure: the object of the habits and rites of which he had spoken were patently going to be the possession of (among other parts of her body) her long thighs concealed beneath the black skirt, her already opened thighs.

Both men were sitting across from her. René was smoking, but before he had lighted his cigarette he had lighted one of those black-hooded lamps which consumes the

71

smoke, and the air, already purified by the wood fire, smelled of the cool odors of the night.

"Will you give me an answer, or would you like to know more?" Sir Stephen repeated.

"If you give your consent," René said, "I'll personally explain to you Sir Stephen's preferences."

"Demands," Sir Stephen corrected.

The hardest thing, O was thinking, was not the question of giving her consent, and she realized that never for a moment did either of them dream that she might refuse; nor, for that matter, did she. The hardest thing was simply to speak. Her lips were burning and her mouth was dry, all her saliva was gone, an anguish both of fear and desire constricted her throat, and her new-found hands were cold and moist. If only she could have closed her eyes. But she could not. Two gazes stalked her eyes, gazes from which she could not—and did not desire to—escape. They drew her toward something she thought she had left behind for a long time, perhaps forever, at Roissy. For since her return, René had taken her only by caresses, and the symbol signifying that she belonged to anyone who knew the secret of her ring had been without consequence: either she had not met anyone who was familiar with the secret, or else those who had had remained silent—the only person she suspected was Jacqueline (and if Jacqueline had been at Roissy, why wasn't she also wearing the ring? Besides, what right did Jacqueline's knowledge of this secret give her over O, and did it, in fact, give her any?). In order to speak, did she have to move? But she could not move of her own free will—an order from them would immediately have made her get up, but this time what they wanted from her was not blind obedience, acquiescence to an order, they wanted her to anticipate orders, to judge herself a slave and surrender herself as

72

such. This, then, is what they called her consent. She remembered that she had never told René anything but "I love you" or "I'm yours." Today it seemed that they wanted her to speak and to agree to, specifically and in detail, what till now she had only tacitly consented to.

Finally she straightened up and, as though what she was going to say was stifling her, unfastened the top hooks of her tunic, until the cleavage of her breasts was visible. Then she stood up. Her hands and her knees were shaking.

"I'm yours," she said at length to René. "I'll be whatever you want me to be."

"No," he broke in, "ours. Repeat after me: I belong to both of you. I shall be whatever both of you want me to be."

Sir Stephen's piercing gray eyes were fixed firmly upon her, as were René's, and in them she was lost, slowly repeating after him the phrases he was dictating to her, but like a lesson of grammar, she was transposing them into the first person.

"To Sir Stephen and to me you grant the right . . ." The right to dispose of her body however they wished, in whatever place or manner they should choose, the right to keep her in chains, the right to whip her like a slave or prisoner for the slightest failing or infraction, or simply for their pleasure, the right to pay no heed to her pleas and cries, if they should make her cry out.

"I believe," said René, "that at this point Sir Stephen would like me to take over, both you and I willing, and have me brief you concerning his demands."

O was listening to her lover, and the words which he had spoken to her at Roissy came back to her: they were almost the same words. But then she had listened snuggled up against him, protected by a feeling of improbability, as though it were all a dream, as though she existed only in another life and perhaps did not really exist at all. Dream or nightmare, the prison setting, the lavish party gowns, men in masks: all this removed her from her own life, even to the point of being uncertain how long it would last. There, at Roissy, she felt the way you do at night, lost in a dream you have had before and are now beginning to dream all over again: certain that it exists and certain that it will end, and you want it to end because you're not sure you'll be able to bear it, and you also want it to go on so you'll know how it comes out. Well, the end was here, where she least expected it (or no longer expected it at all) and in the form she least expected (assuming, she was saying to herself, that this really was the end, that there was not actually another hiding behind this one, and perhaps still another behind the next one). The present end was toppling her from memory into reality and, besides, what had only been reality in a closed circle, a private universe, was suddenly about to contaminate all the customs and circumstances of her daily life, both on her and within her, now no longer satisfied with signs and symbols—the bare buttocks, bodices that unhook, the iron ring—but demanding fulfillment.

It was true that René had never whipped her, and the only difference between the period of their relationship prior to his taking her to Roissy and the time elapsed since her return was that now he used both her backside and mouth the way he formerly had used only her womb (which he continued to use). She had never been able to tell whether the floggings she had regularly received at Roissy had been administered, were it only once, by him (whenever there was any question about it, that is when she herself had been blindfolded or when those with whom she was dealing were masked), but she tended to doubt it.

The pleasure he derived from the spectacle of her body bound and surrendered, struggling vainly, and of her cries, was doubtless so great that he could not bear the idea of lending a hand himself and thus having his attention distracted from it. It was as though he were admitting it, since he was now saying to her, so gently, so tenderly, without moving from the deep armchair in which he was half reclining with his legs crossed, he was saying how happy he was to be turning her over to, how happy he was that she was handing *herself* over to, the commands and desires of Sir Stephen. Whenever Sir Stephen would like her to spend the night at his place, or only an hour, or if he should want her to accompany him outside Paris or, in Paris itself, to join him at some restaurant or for some show, he would telephone her and send his car for her—unless René himself came to pick her up. Today, now, it was her turn to speak. Did she consent? But words failed her. This willful assent they were suddenly asking her to express was the agreement to surrender herself, to say yes in advance to everything to which she most assuredly wanted to say yes but to which her body said no, at least insofar as the whipping was concerned. As for the rest, if she were honest with herself, she would have to admit to a feeling of both anxiety and excitement caused by what she read in Sir Stephen's eyes, a feeling too intense for her to delude herself, and as she was trembling like a leaf, and perhaps for the very reason that she was trembling, she knew that she was waiting more impatiently than he for the moment when he would place his hand, and perhaps his lips, upon her. It was probably up to her to hasten the moment. Whatever courage, or whatever surge of overwhelming desire she may have had, she felt herself suddenly grow so weak as she was about to reply that she slipped to the floor, her dress in full bloom around her, and in the silence Sir Stephen's hollow voice remarked that fear was becoming to her too. His words were not intended for her, but for René. O had the feeling that he was restraining himself from advancing upon her, and regretted his restraint. And yet she avoided his gaze, her eyes fixed upon René, terrified lest he should see what was in her eyes and perhaps deem it a betrayal. And yet it was not a betrayal, for if she were to weigh her desire to belong to Sir Stephen against her belonging to René, she would not have had a second's hesitation: the only reason she was yielding to this desire was that René had allowed her to and, to a certain extent, given her to understand that he was ordering her to. And yet there was still a lingering doubt in her mind as to whether René might not be annoyed to see her acquiesce too quickly or too well. The slightest sign from him would obliterate it immediately. But he made no sign, confining himself to ask her for the third time for an answer. She mumbled:

"I consent to whatever you both desire," and lowered her eyes toward her hands, which were waiting unclasped in the hollows of her knees, then added in a murmur: "I should like to know whether I shall be whipped. . . ."

There was a long pause, during which she regretted twenty times over having asked the question. Then Sir Stephen's voice said slowly:

"From time to time."

Then O heard a match being struck and the sound of glasses: both men were probably helping themselves to another round of whisky. René was leaving O to her own devices. René was saying nothing.

"Even if I agree to it now," she said, "even if I promise now, I couldn't bear it."

"All we ask you to do is submit to it, and, if you scream

or moan, to agree ahead of time that it will be in vain," Sir Stephen went on.

"Oh, please, for pity's sake, not yet!" said O, for Sir Stephen was getting to his feet, René was following suit, he leaned down and took her by the shoulders.

"So give us your answer," he said. "Do you consent?"

Finally she said that she did. Gently he helped her up and, having sat down on the big sofa, made her kneel down alongside him facing the sofa, on which reclined her outstretched arms, her bust, and her head. Her eyes were closed, and an image she had seen several years before flashed across her mind: a strange print portraying a woman kneeling, as she was, before an armchair. The floor was of tile, and in one corner a dog and child were playing. The woman's skirts were raised, and standing close beside her was a man brandishing a handful of switches, ready to whip her. They were all dressed in sixteenth-century clothes, and the print bore a title which she had found disgusting: Family Punishment.

With one hand, René took her wrists in a viselike grip, and with the other lifted her skirts so high that she could feel the muslin lining brush her cheek. He caressed her flanks and drew Sir Stephen's attention to the two dimples that graced them, and the softness of the furrow between her thighs. Then with that same hand he pressed her waist, to accentuate further her buttocks, and ordered her to open her knees wider. She obeyed without saying a word. The honors René was bestowing upon her body, and Sir Stephen's replies, and the coarseness of the terms the men were using so overwhelmed her with a shame as violent as it was unexpected that the desire she had felt to be had by Sir Stephen vanished and she began to wish for the whip as a deliverance, for the pain and screams as a justification. But Sir Stephen's hands pried open her

77

loins, forced the buttocks' portal, retreated, took her again, caressed her until she moaned. She was vanquished, undone, and humiliated that she had moaned.

"I leave you to Sir Stephen," René then said. "Remain the way you are, he'll dismiss you when he sees fit."

How often had she remained like this at Roissy, on her knees, offered to one and all? But then she had always had her hands bound together by the bracelets, a happy prisoner upon whom everything was imposed and from whom nothing was asked. Here it was through her own free will that she remained half-naked, whereas a single gesture, the same that would have sufficed to bring her back to her feet, would also have sufficed to cover her. Her promise bound her as much as had the leather bracelets and chains. Was it only the promise? And however humiliated she was, or rather because she had been humiliated, was it not somehow pleasant to be esteemed only for her humiliation, for the meekness with which she surrendered, for the obedient way in which she opened?

With René gone, Sir Stephen having escorted him to the door, she waited thus alone, motionless, feeling more exposed in the solitude and more prostituted by the wait than she had ever felt before, when they were there. The gray and yellow silk of the sofa was smooth to her cheek; through her nylon stockings she felt, below her knees, the thick wool rug, and along the full length of her left thigh, the warmth from the fireplace hearth, for Sir Stephen had added three logs which were blazing noisily. Above a chest of drawers, an antique clock ticked so quietly that it was only audible when everything around was silent. O listened carefully, thinking how absurd her position was in this civilized, tasteful living room. Through the Venetian blinds could be heard the sleepy rumbling of Paris after midnight. In the light of day, tomorrow morning, would she recognize the spot on the sofa cushion where she had laid her head? Would she ever return, in broad daylight, to this same living room, would she ever be treated in the same way here?

Sir Stephen was apparently in no hurry to return, and O, who had waited so submissively for the strangers at Roissy to take their pleasure, now felt a lump rise in her throat at the idea that in one minute, in ten minutes, he would again put his hands on her. But it was not exactly as she had imagined it.

She heard him open the door and cross the room. He remained for some time with his back to the fire, studying O, then in a near whisper he told her to get up and then sit back down. Surprised, almost embarrassed, she obeyed. He courteously brought her a glass of whisky and a cigarette, both of which she refused. Then she saw that he was in a dressing gown, a very conservative dressing gown of gray homespun—a gray that matched his hair. His hands were long and dry and his flat fingernails, cut short, were very white. He caught her staring, and O blushed: these were indeed the same hands which had seized her body, the hands she now dreaded, and desired. But he did not approach her.

"I'd like you to get completely undressed," he said. "But first simply undo your jacket, without getting up."

O unhooked the large gold hooks and slipped her close-fitting jacket down over her shoulders; then she put it at the other end of the sofa, where her fur, her gloves, and her bag were.

"Caress the tips of your breasts, ever so lightly," Sir Stephen said then, before adding: "You must use a darker rouge, yours is too light."

Taken completely aback, O fondled her nipples with her

79

fingertips and felt them stiffen and rise. She covered them with her palms.

"Oh, no!" Sir Stephen said.

She withdrew her hands and lay back against the back of the couch: her breasts were heavy for so slender a torso, and, parting, rose gently toward her armpits. The nape of her neck was resting against the back of the sofa, and her hands were lying on either side of her hips. Why did Sir Stephen not bend over, bring his mouth close to hers, why did his hands not move toward the nipples which he had seen stiffen and which she, being absolutely motionless, could feel quiver whenever she took a breath. But he had drawn near, had sat down across the arm of the sofa, and was not touching her. He was smoking, and a movement of his hand—O never knew whether or not it was voluntary—flicked some still-warm ashes down between her breasts. She had the feeling he wanted to insult her, by his disdain, his silence, by a certain attitude of detachment. Yet he had desired her a while ago, he still did now, she could see it by the tautness beneath the soft material of his dressing gown. Then let him take her, if only to wound her! O hated herself for her own desire, and loathed Sir Stephen for the self control he was displaying. She wanted him to love her, there, the truth was out: she wanted him to be chafing under the urge to touch her lips and penetrate her body, to devastate her if need be, but not to remain so calm and self-possessed. At Roissy, she had not cared in the slightest whether those who used her had had any feeling whatsoever: they were the instruments by which her lover derived pleasure from her, by which she became what he wanted her to be, polished and smooth and gentle as a stone. Their hands were his hands, their orders his orders. But not here. René had turned her over to Sir Stephen, but it was clear that he wanted to share

80

her with him, not to obtain anything further from her, nor
for the pleasure of surrendering her, but in order to share
with Sir Stephen what today he loved most, as no doubt
in days gone by, when they were young, they had shared
a trip, a boat, a horse. And today, this sharing derived its
meaning from René's relation to Sir Stephen much more
than it did from his relation to her. What each of them
would look for in her would be the other's mark, the trace
of the other's passage. Only a short while before, when
she had been kneeling half-naked before René, and Sir
Stephen had opened her thighs with both his hands, René
had explained to Sir Stephen why O's buttocks were so
easily accessible, and why he was pleased that they had
been thus prepared: it was because it had occurred to him
that Sir Stephen would enjoy having his preferred path
constantly at his disposal. He had even added that, if Sir
Stephen wished, he would grant him the sole use of it.

"Why, gladly," Sir Stephen had said, but he had remarked that, in spite of everything, there was a risk he
might rend O.

"O is yours," René had replied, "O will be pleased to be
rent."

And he had leaned down over her and kissed her hands.

The very idea that René could imagine giving up any
part of her left O stunned. She had taken it as the sign
that her lover cared more about Sir Stephen than he did
about her. And too, although he had so often told her that
what he loved in her was the object he had made of her,
her absolute availability to him, his freedom with respect
to her, as one is free to dispose of a piece of furniture,
which one enjoys giving as much as, and sometimes even
more than, one may enjoy keeping it for oneself, she realized that she had not believed him completely.

She saw another sign of what could scarcely be termed

anything but a certain deference or respect toward Sir Stephen, in the fact that René, who so passionately loved to see her beneath the bodies or the blows of others besides himself, whose look was one of constant tenderness, of unflagging gratitude whenever he saw her mouth open to moan or scream, her eyes closed over tears, had left her after having made certain, by exposing her to him, by opening her as one opens a horse's mouth to prove that it is young enough, that Sir Stephen found her beautiful enough or, strictly speaking, suitable enough for him, and vouchsafed to accept her. However offensive and insulting his conduct may have been, O's love for René remained unchanged. She considered herself fortunate to count enough in his eyes for him to derive pleasure from offending her, as believers give thanks to God for humbling them.

But, in Sir Stephen, she thought she detected a will of ice and iron, which would not be swayed by desire, a will in whose judgment, no matter how moving and submissive she might be, she counted for absolutely nothing, at least till now. Otherwise why should she have been so frightened? The whip at the valets' belt at Roissy, the chains borne almost constantly had seemed to her less terrifying than the equanimity of Sir Stephen's gaze as it fastened on the breasts he refrained from touching. She realized to what extent their very fullness, smooth and distended on her tiny shoulders and slender torso, rendered them fragile. She could not keep them from trembling, she would have had to stop breathing. To hope that this fragility would disarm Sir Stephen was futile, and she was fully aware that it was quite the contrary: her proffered gentleness cried for wounds as much as caresses, fingernails as much as lips. She had a momentary illusion: Sir Stephen's right hand, which was holding his cigarette, grazed their tips with the end of his middle finger and, obediently, they stiffened further. That this, for Sir Stephen, was a game, or the guise of a game, nothing more, or a check, the way one checks to ascertain whether a machine is functioning properly, O had no doubt.

Without moving from the arm of his chair, Sir Stephen then told her to take off her skirt. O's moist hands made the hooks slippery, and it took her two tries before she succeeded in undoing the black faille petticoat under her skirt.

When she was completely naked, her high-heeled patent-leather sandals and her black nylon stockings rolled down flat above her knees, accentuating the delicate lines of her legs and the whiteness of her thighs, Sir Stephen, who had also gotten to his feet, seized her loins with one hand and pushed her toward the sofa. He had her kneel down, her back against the sofa, and to make her press more tightly against it with her shoulders than with her waist, he made her spread her thighs slightly. Her hands were lying on her ankles, thus forcing her belly ajar, and above her still proffered breasts, her throat arched back.

She did not dare look Sir Stephen in the face, but she saw his hands undoing his belt. When he had straddled O, who was still kneeling, and had seized her by the nape of the neck, he drove into her mouth. It was not the caress of her lips the length of him he was looking for, but the back of her throat. For a long time he probed, and O felt the suffocating gag of flesh swell and harden, its slow repeated hammering finally bringing her to tears. In order to invade her better, Sir Stephen ended by kneeling on the sofa, one knee on each side of her face, and there were moments when his buttocks rested on O's breast, and in her heart she felt her womb, useless and scorned, burning her. Although he delighted and reveled in her for a long time, Sir Stephen did not bring his pleasure to a climax, but withdrew from her in silence and rose again to his feet, without closing his dressing gown.

"You are easy, O," he said to her. "You love René, but you're easy. Does René realize that you covet and long for all the men who desire you, that by sending you to Roissy or surrendering you to others he is providing you with a string of alibis to cover your easy virtue?"

"I love René," O replied.

"You love René, but you desire me, among others," Sir Stephen went on.

Yes, she did desire him, but what if René, upon learning it, were to change? All she could do was remain silent and lower her eyes: even to have looked Sir Stephen directly in the eyes would have been tantamount to a confession.

Then Sir Stephen bent down over her and, taking her by the shoulders, made her slide down onto the rug. Again she was on her back, her legs raised and doubled up against her. Sir Stephen, who had sat down on that part of the couch against which she had just been leaning, seized her right knee and pulled her toward him. Since she was facing the fireplace, the light from the nearby hearth shed a fierce light upon the double, quartered furrow of her belly and rear. Without loosing his grip, Sir Stephen abruptly ordered her to caress herself, without closing her legs. Startled, O meekly stretched her right hand toward her loins, where her fingers encountered the ridge of flesh —already emerging from the protective fleece beneath, already burning—where her belly's fragile lips merged.

But her hand recoiled and she mumbled:

"I can't."

And in fact she could not. The only times she had ever caressed herself furtively had been in the warmth and obscurity of her bed, when she slept alone, but she had never tried to carry it to a climax. But later she would sometimes come upon it in her sleep and would wake up disappointed that it had been so intense and yet so fleeting.

Sir Stephen's gaze was persistent. She could not bear it, and repeating "I can't," she closed her eyes.

What she was seeing in her mind's eye, what she had never been able to forget, what still filled her with the same sensation of nausea and disgust that she had felt when she had first witnessed it when she was fifteen, was the image of Marion slumped in the leather armchair in a hotel room, Marion with one leg sprawled over one arm of the chair and her head half hanging over the other, caressing herself in her, O's, presence, and moaning. Marion had related to her how she had one day caressed herself this way in her office when she had thought she was alone, and her boss had happened to walk in and caught her in the act.

O remembered Marion's office, a bare room with pale green walls, with the north light filtering in through dusty windows. There was only one easy chair, intended for visitors, facing the table.

"Did you run away?" O had asked.

"No," Marion had answered, "he asked me to begin all over again, but he locked the door, made me take off my panties, and pushed the chair over in front of the window."

O had been overwhelmed with admiration—and with horror—for what she took to be Marion's courage, and had steadfastly refused to fondle herself in Marion's presence and sworn that she never would, in anyone's presence. Marion had laughed and said:

"You'll see. Wait till your lover asks you to."

René never had asked her to. Would she have obeyed? Yes, of course she would, but she would also have been terrified at the thought that she might see René's eyes filling with the same disgust that she had felt for Marion. Which was absurd. And since it was Sir Stephen, it was all the more absurd; what did she care whether Sir Stephen was disgusted? But no, she couldn't. For the third time she murmured:

"I can't."

Though she uttered the words in almost a whisper, he heard them, let her go, rose to his feet, closed his dressing gown, and ordered O to get up.

"Is this your obedience?" he said.

Then he caught both her wrists with his left hand, and with his right he slapped her on both sides of the face. She staggered, and would have fallen had he not held her up.

"Kneel down and listen to me," he said. "I'm afraid René's training leaves a great deal to be desired."

"I always obey René," she mumbled.

"You're confusing love and obedience. You'll obey me without loving me, and without my loving you."

With that, she felt a strange inexplicable storm of revolt rising within her, silently denying in the depths of her being the words she was hearing, denying her promises of submission and slavery, denying her own agreement, her own desire, her nakedness, her sweat, her trembling limbs, the circles under her eyes. She struggled and clenched her teeth with rage when, having made her bend over, with her elbows on the floor and her head between her arms, her buttocks raised, he forced her from behind, to rend her as René had said he would.

The first time she did not cry out. He went at it again, harder now, and she screamed. She screamed as much out of revolt as of pain, and he was fully aware of it. She also

knew—which meant that in any event she was vanquished
—that he was pleased to make her cry out. When he had
finished with her, and after he had helped her to her feet,
he was on the point of dismissing her when he remarked
to her that what he had spilled in her was going to seep
slowly out tinted with the blood of the wound he had inflicted on her, that this wound would burn her as long as
her buttocks were not used to him and he was obliged to
keep on forcing his way. René had reserved this particular
use of her to him, and he certainly intended to make full
use of it, she had best have no illusions on that score.
He reminded her that she had agreed to be René's slave,
and his too, but that it appeared unlikely that she was
aware—consciously aware—of what she had consented
to. By the time she had learned, it would be too late for
her to escape.

Listening, O told herself that perhaps it would also be
too late for him to escape becoming enamored of her, for
she had no intention of being quickly tamed, and by the
time she was he might have learned to love her a little.
For all her inner resistance, and the timid refusal she had
dared to display, had one object and one object alone: she
wanted to exist for Sir Stephen, in however modest a way,
in the same way she existed for René, and wanted him to
feel something more than desire for her. Not that she was
in love, but because she clearly saw that René loved Sir
Stephen in that passionate way boys love their elders, and
she sensed that he was ready, if need be, to sacrifice her
to any and all of Sir Stephen's whims, in an effort to
satisfy him. She knew with an infallible intuition that
René would follow Sir Stephen's example and emulate his
attitude, and that if Sir Stephen were to show contempt
for her, René would be contaminated by it, no matter how
much he loved her, contaminated in a way he had never

87

before been, or had dreamed of being, by the opinions and example of the men at Roissy. This was because at Roissy, with regard to her, he was the master, and the opinions of all the men there to whom he gave her derived from and depended on his own. Here he was not the master any longer. On the contrary. Sir Stephen was René's master, without René's being fully aware of it, which is to say that René admired him and wanted to emulate him, to compete with him, and this was why he was sharing everything with him, and why he had given O to him: this time it was apparent that she had been given with no strings attached. René would probably go on loving her insofar as Sir Stephen deemed that she was worth the trouble and would love her himself. Till then, it was clear that Sir Stephen would be her master and, regardless of what René might think, her only master, in the precise relationship of master to slave. She did not expect any pity from him; but could she not hope to wrest some slight feeling of love from him?

Sprawled in the same big armchair, next to the fire, which he had been occupying before René's departure, he had left her standing there naked and told her to await his further orders. She had waited without saying a word. Then he had got to his feet and told her to follow him. Still naked, except for her high-heeled sandals and black stockings, she had followed him up a flight of stairs which went from the ground-floor landing, and entered a small bedroom, a room so tiny there was only space enough for a bed in one corner and a dressing table and chair between the bed and window. This small room communicated with a larger room, which was Sir Stephen's, with a common bathroom between.

O washed and wiped herself—the towel was faintly stained with pink—removed her sandals and stockings, and crawled in between the cold sheets. The curtains of the window were open, but the night was dark.

Before he closed the door between their rooms, after O was already in bed, Sir Stephen came over to her and kissed her fingertips, as he had done when she had slipped down off her stool in the bar and he had complimented her on her iron ring. Thus, he had thrust his hands and sex into her, ransacked and ravaged her mouth and rear, but condescended only to place his lips upon her fingertips. O wept, and did not fall asleep until dawn.

The following day, a little before noon, Sir Stephen's chauffeur drove O home. She had awakened at ten, an elderly mulatto servant had brought her a cup of coffee, prepared her bath, and given her her clothes, except for her fur wrap, her gloves, and her bag, which she had found on the living-room couch when she had gone downstairs. The living room was empty, the Venetian blinds were raised, and the curtains were open. Through the window opposite the couch, she could see a garden green and narrow as an aquarium, planted in nothing but ivy, holly, and spindle hedges.

As she was putting on her coat, the mulatto servant told her that Sir Stephen had left, and handed her an envelope on which there was nothing but her initial; the white sheet inside consisted of two lines: "René phoned that he would come by for you at the studio at six o'clock," signed with an S and with a postscript: "The riding crop is for your next visit."

O glanced around her: on the table, between the two chairs in which Sir Stephen and René had been sitting the evening before, there was a long, slender, leather riding crop near a vase of yellow roses. The servant was waiting at the door. O put the letter in her bag and left.

So René had phoned Sir Stephen, and not her. Back home, after having taken off her clothes, and having had lunch in her dressing gown, she still had plenty of time to freshen her make-up and rearrange her hair, and to get dressed to go to the studio, where she was due at three o'clock. The telephone did not ring; René did not call her. Why? What had Sir Stephen told him? How had they talked about her? She remembered the words they both had used in her presence, their casual remarks concerning the advantages of her body with respect to the demands of theirs. Perhaps it was merely that she was not used to this kind of vocabulary in English, but the only French equivalents she could find seemed utterly base and contemptible to her. It was true that she had been passed from hand to hand as often as were the prostitutes in brothels, so why should they treat her otherwise? "I love you, I love you René," she repeated, softly calling to him in the solitude of her room, "I love you, do whatever you want with me, but don't leave me, for God's sake don't leave me."

Who pities those who wait? They are easily recognized: by their gentleness, by their falsely attentive looks—attentive, yes, but to something other than what they are looking at—by their absent-mindedness. For three long hours, in the studio where a short, plump red-haired model whom O did not know and who was modeling hats for her, O was that absent-minded person, withdrawn into herself by her desire for the minutes to hasten by, and by her own anxiety.

Over a blouse and petticoat of red silk she had put on a plaid skirt and a short suede jacket. The bright red of her blouse beneath her partly opened jacket made her already pale face seem even paler, and the little red-haired model told her that she looked like a femme fatale. "Fatal for whom?" O said to herself.

Two years earlier, before she had met and fallen in love with René, she would have sworn: "Fatal for Sir Stephen" and have added: "and he'll know it too." But her love for René and René's love for her had stripped her of all her weapons, and instead of providing her with any new proof of her power, had stripped her of those she had previously possessed. Once she had been indifferent and fickle, someone who enjoyed tempting, by a word or gesture, the boys who were in love with her, but without giving them anything, then giving herself impulsively, for no reason, once and only once, as a reward, but also to inflame them even more and render a passion she did not share even more cruel. She was sure that they loved her. One of them had tried to commit suicide; when he had been released from the hospital where they had taken him, she had gone to his place, had stripped naked, and forbidding him to touch her, had lain down on his couch. Pale with pain and passion, he had stared at her silently for two hours, petrified by the promise he had made. She had never wanted to see him again. It wasn't that she took lightly the desire she aroused. She understood it, or thought she understood, all the more so because she herself felt a similar desire (or so she thought) for her girl friends, or for young strangers, girls she encountered by chance. Some of them yielded to her, and she would take them to some discreet hotel with its narrow hallways and paper-thin walls, while others, horrified, spurned her. But what she took—or mistook—to be desire was actually nothing more than the thirst for conquest, and neither her tough-guy exterior nor the fact that she had had several lovers—if you could call them lovers—nor her hardness, nor even her courage was of any help to her when she met

René. In the space of a week she learned fear, but certainty; anguish, but happiness. René threw himself at her like a pirate at his prisoner, and she reveled in her captivity, feeling on her wrists, her ankles, feeling on all her members and in the secret depths of her heart and body, bonds less visible than the finest strands of hair, more powerful than the cables the Lilliputians used to tie up Gulliver, bonds her lover loosened or tightened with a glance. She was no longer free? Yes! thank God, she was no longer free. But she was light, a nymph on clouds, a fish in water, lost in happiness. Lost because these fine strands of hair, these cables which René held, without exception, in his hand, were the only network through which the current of life any longer flowed into her.

This was true to such a degree that when René relaxed his grip upon her—or when she imagined he had—when he seemed distracted, when he left her in a mood which she took to be indifference or let some time go by without seeing her or replying to her letters and she assumed that he no longer cared to see her and was on the verge of ceasing to love her, then everything was choked and smothered within her. The grass turned black, day was no longer day nor night any longer night, but both merely infernal machines which alternately provided, as part of her torture, periods of light and darkness. Cool water made her nauseous. She felt as though she were a statue of ashes—bitter, useless, damned—like the salt statues of Gomorrah. For she was guilty. Those who love God, and by Him are abandoned in the dark of night, are guilty, *because* they are abandoned. They cast back into their memories, searching for their sins. She looked back, hunting for hers. All she found were insignificant acts of kindness or self-indulgence, which were not so much acts as an innate part of her personality, such as arousing the

92

desires of men other than René, men she noticed only to the extent that the love René gave her, the certainty of belonging to René, made her happy and filled her cup of happiness to overflowing, and insofar as her total submission to René rendered her vulnerable, irresponsible, and all her trifling acts—but what acts? For all she had to reproach herself with were thoughts and fleeting temptations. Yet, he was certain that she was guilty and, without really wanting to, René was punishing her for a sin he knew nothing about (since it remained completely internal), although Sir Stephen had immediately detected it: her wantonness.

O was happy that René had had her whipped and had prostituted her, because her impassioned submission would furnish her lover with the proof that she belonged to him, but also because the pain and shame of the lash, and the outrage inflicted upon her by those who compelled her to pleasure when they took her, and at the same time delighted in their own without paying the slightest heed to hers, seemed to her the very redemption of her sins. There had been embraces she had found foul, hands that had been an intolerable insult on her breasts, mouths which had sucked in her lips and tongue like so many soft, vile leeches, and tongues and sexes, viscous beasts which, caressing themselves at her closed mouth, at the double furrow, before and behind, which she had squeezed tight with all her might, had stiffened her with disgust and kept her stiffened so long that it was all the whip could do to unbend her, but she had finally yielded to the blows and opened, with disgust and abominable servility. And what if, in spite of that, Sir Stephen was right? What if she actually enjoyed her debasement? In that case, the baser she was, the more merciful was René to consent to make O the instrument of his pleasure.

93

As a child, O had read a Biblical text in red letters on the white wall of a room in Wales where she had lived for two months, a text such as the Protestants often inscribe in their houses:

IT IS A FEARFUL THING TO FALL
INTO THE HANDS OF THE LIVING GOD

No, O told herself now, that isn't true. What is fearful is to be cast out of the hands of the living God. Every time René postponed, or was late to, a rendezvous with her, as he had done today—for six o'clock had come and gone, as had six-thirty—O was prey to a dual feeling of madness and despair, but for nothing. Madness for nothing, despair for nothing, nothing was true. René would arrive, he would be there, nothing was changed, he loved her but had been held up by a staff meeting or some extra work, he had not had time to let her know; in a flash, O emerged from her airless chamber, and yet each of these attacks of terror would leave behind, somewhere deep inside her, a dull premonition, a warning of woe: for there were also times when René neglected to let her know when the reason for the delay was a game of golf or a hand of bridge, or perhaps another face, for he loved O but he was free, sure of her and fickle, so fickle. Would a day of death and ashes not come, a day in the long string of other days which would give the nod to madness, a day when the gas chamber would reopen? Oh, let the miracle continue, let me still be touched by grace, René don't leave me! Each day, O did not look, nor did she care to look, any further than the next day and the day after; nor, each week, any further than the following week. And for her every night with René was a night which would last forever.

René finally arrived at seven, so happy to see her again that he kissed her in front of the electrician who was repairing a floodlight, in front of the short, red-haired model who was just coming out of the dressing room, and in front of Jacqueline, whom no one expected, who had come in suddenly on the heels of the other model.

"What a lovely sight," Jacqueline said to O. "I was just passing, I wanted to ask you for the last shots of me you took, but I gather this isn't the right moment. I'll be on my way."

"Mademoiselle, please don't go," René called after her, without letting go of O, whom he was holding around the waist, "please don't go!"

O introduced them: Jacqueline, René; René, Jacqueline.

Piqued, the red-haired model had gone back into her dressing room, the electrician was pretending to be busy. O was looking at Jacqueline and could feel René's eyes following her gaze. Jacqueline was wearing a ski outfit, the kind that only movie stars who never go skiing wear. Her black sweater accentuated her small, widely spaced breasts, her tight-fitting ski pants did the same for her long, winter-sports-girl legs. Everything about her looked like snow: the bluish sheen of her gray sealskin jacket was snow in the shade; the hoar-frost reflection of her hair and eyelashes, snow in sunlight. She had on lipstick whose deep red shaded almost to purple, and when she smiled and lifted her eyes till they were fixed on O, O said to herself that no one could resist the desire to drink of that green and moving water beneath the silvery lashes, to rip off her sweater to lay his hands on the fairly small breasts. There, you see: no sooner had René returned than, completely reassured by his presence, she recovered her taste for others and for herself, her zest for life itself.

They left together, all three of them. On the rue Royale the snow, which had been falling in large flakes for two hours, fell now in eddies of thin little white flies which stung the face. The rock salt scattered on the sidewalk crunched beneath their feet and melted the snow, and O felt the icy breath it emitted rising along her legs and fasten on her naked thighs.

O had a fairly clear idea of what she was looking for in the young women she pursued. It wasn't that she wanted to give the impression she was vying with men, nor that she was trying to compensate by her manifest masculinity for a female inferiority which she in no wise felt. It's true that when she was twenty she had caught herself courting the prettiest of her girl friends by doffing her beret, by standing aside to let her pass, and by offering a hand to help her out of a taxi. In the same vein, she would not tolerate not paying whenever they had tea together in some pastry shop. She would kiss her hand and, if she had a chance, her mouth, if possible in the street. But these were so many affectations she paraded for the sake of scandal, displayed much more from childishness than from conviction. On the other hand, her penchant for the sweetness of sweetly made-up lips yielding beneath her own, for the porcelain or pearly sparkle of eyes half-closed in the half-light of couches at five in the afternoon, when the curtains are drawn and the lamp on the fireplace mantel lighted, for the voices that say: "Again, oh, please, again . . . ," for the marine odor clinging to her fingers: this was a real, deeply-rooted taste. And she also enjoyed the pursuit just as much. Probably not for the pursuit itself, however amusing or fascinating it might be, but for the complete sense of freedom she experienced in the act of hunting. She, and she alone, set the rules and directed the proceedings (something she never did with men, or only in a most oblique manner). She initiated the discussions and set the rendezvous, the kisses came from her too, so much so that she preferred not to have someone kiss her first, and since she had first had lovers she almost never allowed the girl whom she was caressing to return her caresses. As much as she was in a hurry to behold her girl friend naked, she was equally quick to find excuses why she herself should not undress. She often looked for excuses to avoid it, saying that she was cold, that it was the wrong time of the month for her. And, what is more, rare was the woman in whom she failed to detect some element of beauty. She remembered that, just out of the *lycée*, she had tried to seduce an ugly, disagreeable, constantly ill-natured little girl for the sole reason that she had a wild mop of blond hair which, by its unevenly cut curls, created a forest of light and shade over a skin that, while lusterless, had a texture which was soft, smooth, and totally flat. But the little girl had repelled her advances, and if one day pleasure had ever lighted up the ungrateful wench's face, it had not been because of O. For O passionately loved to see faces enveloped in that mist which makes them so young and smooth, a timeless youth that does not restore childhood but enlarges the lips, widens the eyes the way makeup does, and renders the iris sparkling and clear. In this, admiration played a larger part than pride, for it was not her handiwork which moved her: at Roissy she had experienced the same uncomfortable feeling in the presence of the transfigured face of a girl possessed by a stranger. The nakedness and surrender of the bodies overwhelmed her, and she had the feeling that her girl friends, when they simply agreed to display themselves naked in a locked room, were giving her a gift which she could never repay in kind. For the nakedness of vacations, in the sun and on the beaches, made no impression on her—not simply because it was public but because, being public and not absolute, she was to some extent protected from it. The beauty of other women, which with unfailing generosity she was inclined to find superior to her own, nevertheless reassured her concerning her own beauty, in which she saw, whenever she unexpectedly caught a glimpse of herself in a mirror, a kind of reflection of theirs. The power she acknowledged that her girl friends held over her was at the same time a guarantee of her own power over men. And what she asked of women (and never returned, or ever so little), she was happy and found it quite natural that men should be eager and impatient to ask of her. Thus was she constantly and simultaneously the accomplice of both men and women, having, as it were, her cake and eating it too. There were times when the game was not all that easy. That O was in love with Jacqueline, no more and no less than she had been in love with many others, and assuming that the term "in love" (which was saying a great deal) was the proper one, there could be no doubt. But why did she conceal it so?

When the buds burst open on the poplar trees along the quays, and daylight, lingering longer, gave lovers time to sit for a while in the gardens after work, she thought she had at last found the courage to face Jacqueline. In winter, Jacqueline had seemed too triumphant to her beneath her cool furs, too iridescent, untouchable, inaccessible. And Jacqueline knew it. Spring put her back into suits, flat-heeled shoes, sweaters. With her short Dutch bob, she finally resembled those fresh school girls whom O, as a *lycée* student herself, used to grab by the wrists and drag silently into an empty cloakroom and push back against the hanging coats. The coats would tumble from the hangers. Then O would burst out laughing. They used to wear uniform blouses of raw cotton, with their initials

embroidered in red cotton on their breast pockets. Three
years later, three kilometers away, Jacqueline had worn
the same blouses in another *lycée.* It was by chance that
O learned that one day when Jacqueline was modeling
some high-fashion dresses and said with a sigh that, really,
if only they had had as pretty dresses at school, they would
have been much happier there. Or if they had been allowed to wear the jumper they gave you, without anything on underneath. "What do you mean, without anything on?" O said. "Without a dress, naturally," Jacqueline
replied. To which O began to blush. She could not get
used to being naked beneath her dress, and any equivocal
remark seemed to her to be an allusion to her condition.
It did no good to keep on repeating to herself that one is
always naked beneath one's clothes. No, she felt as naked
as that woman from Verona who went out to offer herself
to the chief of the besieging army in order to free her city:
naked beneath a coat, which only needed to be opened a
crack. It also seemed to her that, like the Italian, her
nakedness was meant to redeem something. But what?
Since Jacqueline was sure of herself, she had nothing to
redeem; she had no need to be reassured, all she needed
was a mirror. O looked at her humbly, thinking that the
only flowers one could offer her were magnolias, because
their thick, lusterless petals slowly turn to bister as they
fade and wither, or else camellias, because their waxen
whiteness is sometimes infused with a pink glow. As
winter waned, the pale tan that gilded Jacqueline's skin
vanished with the memory of the snow. Soon, only camellias would do. But O was afraid of making a fool of
herself with these melodramatic flowers. One day she
brought a big bouquet of blue hyacinths, whose odor is
overwhelming, like that of tuberoses: oily, cloying, clinging, exactly the odor camellias ought to have but don't.

Jacqueline buried her Mongolian nose in the warm, stiff-stemmed flowers, her small nose and her pink lips, for she had been wearing a pink lipstick for the past two weeks, and not red any longer.

"Are they for me?" she said, the way women do who are used to receiving gifts.

Then she thanked O and asked her if René were coming for her. Yes, he was coming, O said. He's coming, she repeated to herself; and it will be for him that Jacqueline will lift her icy, liquid eyes for a second, those eyes which never look at anyone squarely, as she stands there falsely motionless, falsely silent. No one would need to teach her anything: neither to remain silent nor how to keep her hands unclenched at her sides, nor indeed how to arch her head half back. O was dying to seize a handful of that too blond hair at the nape of the neck, and pull her docile head all the way back, to run at least her finger over the line of her eyebrows. But René would want to do it too.

She was fully aware why she, once so daring and bold, had become so shy, why she had wanted Jacqueline for two months without betraying it by the least word or gesture, and giving herself lame excuses to explain her timidity. It was not true that Jacqueline was intangible. The obstacle was not in Jacqueline, it lay deep within O herself, its roots deeper than anything she had ever before encountered. It was because René was leaving her free, and because she loathed her freedom. Her freedom was worse than any chains. Her freedom was separating her from René. She could have taken Jacqueline by the shoulders any number of times and, without saying a word, pinned her against the wall with her two hands, the way a butterfly is impaled; Jacqueline would not have moved, and probably not even done so much as smile. But O was henceforth like those wild animals which have been taken

100

captive and either serve as decoys for the hunter or, leaping forward only at the hunter's command, head off the game for him.

It was she who sometimes leaned back against a wall, pale and trembling, stubbornly impaled by her silence, bound there by her silence, so happy to remain silent. She was waiting for more than permission, since she already had permission. She was waiting for an order. It came to her not from René, but from Sir Stephen.

As the months went by since the day René had given her to Sir Stephen, O was terrified to note the growing importance Sir Stephen was assuming in her lover's eyes. Moreover, she realized at the same time that, in this matter, she was perhaps mistaken, imagining a progression in the fact or the feeling where actually the only progression had been in the acknowledgment of this fact or the admission of this feeling. Be that as it may, she had been quick to note that René chose to spend with her those nights, and only those nights, following those she had spent with Sir Stephen (Sir Stephen keeping her the whole night only when René was away from Paris). She also noticed that when René remained for one of those evenings at Sir Stephen's he would never touch O except to make her more readily available or an easier offering to Sir Stephen, if she happened to be struggling. It was extremely rare for him to stay, and he never did unless at Sir Stephen's express request. Whenever he did, he remained fully dressed, as he had done the first time, keeping quiet, lighting one cigarette after another, adding wood to the fire, serving Sir Stephen something to drink—but not drinking himself. O felt that he was watching her the way a lion trainer watches the animal he has trained, careful to see that it performs with complete obedience and thus does honor to him, but even more the way a prince's bodyguard or a bandit's second-in-command keeps an eye on the prostitute he has gone down to fetch in the street. The proof that he was indeed yielding to the role of servant or acolyte resided in the fact that he watched Sir Stephen's face more closely than he did hers —and beneath his gaze O felt herself stripped of the very voluptuousness in which her features were immersed: for this sensual pleasure René paid obeisance, expressed admiration and even gratitude to Sir Stephen, who had engendered it, pleased that he had deigned to take pleasure in something he had given him.

Everything would probably have been much simpler if Sir Stephen had liked boys, and O did not doubt that René, who was not so inclined, still would have readily granted to Sir Stephen both the slightest and the most demanding of his requests. But Sir Stephen only liked women.

O realized that through the medium of her body, shared between them, they attained something more mysterious and perhaps more acute, more intense than an amorous communion, the very conception of which was arduous but whose reality and force she could not deny. Still, why was this division in a way abstract? At Roissy, O had, at the same time and in the same place, belonged both to René and to other men. Why did René, in Sir Stephen's presence, refrain not only from taking her, but from giving her any orders? (All he ever did was pass on Sir Stephen's.) She asked him why, certain beforehand of the reply.

"Out of respect," René replied.

"But I belong to *you*," O said.

"You belong to Sir Stephen *first*."

And it was true, at least in the sense that when René had surrendered her to his friend the surrender had been absolute, that Sir Stephen's slightest desires took precedence over René's decisions as far as she was concerned, and even over her own. If René had decided that they would dine together and go to the theater, and Sir Stephen happened to phone an hour before he was to pick up O, René would come by for her at the studio as agreed, but only to drive her to Sir Stephen's door and leave her there. Once, and only once, O had asked René to please ask Sir Stephen to change the day, because she so much wanted to go with René to a party to which they were both invited. René had refused.

"My sweet angel," he had said, "you mean you still haven't understood that you no longer belong to me, that I'm no longer the master who's in charge of you?"

Not only had he refused, but he had told Sir Stephen of O's request and, in her presence, asked him to punish her harshly enough so that she would never again dare even to conceive of shirking her duties.

"Certainly," Sir Stephen had replied.

The scene had taken place in the little oval room with the inlaid floor, in which the only piece of furniture was a table encrusted with mother-of-pearl, the room adjoining the yellow and gray living room. René remained only long enough to betray O and hear Sir Stephen's reply. Then he shook hands with him, smiled at O, and left. Through the window, O saw him crossing the courtyard; he did not turn around; she heard the car door slam shut, the roar of the motor, and in a little mirror imbedded in the wall she caught a glimpse of her own image: she was white with fear and despair. Then, mechanically, when she walked past Sir Stephen, who opened the living-room door for her and stood back for her to pass, she looked at him: he was as pale as she. In a flash, she was absolutely certain that he loved her, but it was a fleeting certainty that vanished as fast as it had come. Although she did not believe it and chided herself for having thought of it, she was comforted by it and undressed meekly, on a mere signal from him. Then, and for the first time since he had been making her come two or three times a week, and using her slowly, sometimes making her wait for an hour naked without coming near her, listening to her entreaties without ever replying, for there were times when she did beg and beseech, enjoining her to do the same things always at the same moments, as in a ritual, so that she knew when her mouth was supposed to caress him and when, on her knees, her head buried in the silken sofa, she should offer him only her back, which he now possessed without hurting her, for the first time, for in spite of the fear which convulsed her—or perhaps because of that fear—she opened to him, in spite of the chagrin she felt at René's betrayal, but perhaps too because of it, she surrendered herself completely. And for the first time, so gentle were her yielding eyes when they fastened on Sir Stephen's pale, burning gaze, that he suddenly spoke to her in French, employing the familiar *tu* form with her:

"I'm going to put a gag in your mouth, O, because I'd like to whip you till I draw blood. Do I have your permission?"

"I'm yours," O said.

She was standing in the middle of the drawing room, and her arms, raised and held together by the Roissy bracelets, which were attached by a chain to a ring in the ceiling from which a chandelier had formerly hung, thrust her breasts forward. Sir Stephen caressed them, then kissed them, then kissed her mouth, once, ten times. (He had never kissed her.) And when he had put on the gag, which filled her mouth with the taste of wet canvas and pushed her tongue to the back of her throat, the gag so arranged that she could scarcely clench it in her teeth, he took her gently by the hair. Held in equilibrium by the chain, she stumbled on her bare feet.

"Excuse me, O," he murmured (he had never before begged her pardon), then he let her go, and struck.

When René returned to O's apartment after midnight, after having gone alone to the party they had intended to go to together, he found her in bed, trembling in the white nylon of her long nightgown. Sir Stephen had brought her home and put her to bed himself and kissed her again. She told René that. She also told him that she no longer had any inclination not to obey Sir Stephen, realizing full well that from this René would conclude that she deemed it essential, and even pleasant, to be beaten (which was true; but this was not the only reason). What she was also certain of was that it was equally essential to René that she be beaten. He was as horrified at the idea of striking her—so much so that he had never been able to bring himself to do it—as he enjoyed seeing her struggle and hearing her scream. Once, in his presence, Sir Stephen had used the riding crop on her. René had forced O back against the table and held her there, motionless. Her skirt had slipped down; he had lifted it up. Perhaps he needed even more to know that while he was not with her, while he was away walking or working, O was writhing, moaning, and crying beneath the whip, was asking for his pity and not obtaining it—and was aware that this pain and humiliation had been inflicted on her by the will of the lover whom she loved, and for his pleasure. At Roissy, he had had her flogged by the valets. In Sir Stephen he had found the stern master he himself was unable to be. The fact that the man he most admired in the world could take a fancy to her and take the trouble to tame her, only made René's passion all the greater, as O could plainly see. All the mouths that had probed her mouth, all the hands that had seized her breasts and her belly, all the members that had been thrust into her and so perfectly provided the living proof that she was indeed prostituted, had at the same time provided the proof that she was worthy of being prostituted and had, so to speak, sanctified her. But this, in René's eyes, was nothing compared to the proof Sir Stephen provided. Each time she emerged from his arms, René looked for the mark of a god upon her. O knew full well that if he had betrayed her a few hours before, it was in order to provoke new, and more cruel, marks. And she also knew that, though the reasons for provoking them might disappear, Sir Stephen would not turn back. So much the worse. (But to herself she was thinking the exact opposite.) René, impressed and overwhelmed, gazed for a long time at the thin body marked by thick, purple welts like so many ropes spanning the shoulders, the back, the buttocks, the belly, and the breasts, welts which sometimes overlapped and crisscrossed. Here and there a little blood still oozed.

"Oh, how I love you," he murmured.

With trembling hands he took off his clothes, turned out the light, and lay down next to O. She moaned in the darkness, all the time he possessed her.

The welts on O's body took almost a month to disappear. In places where the skin had been broken, she still bore the traces of slightly whiter lines, like very old scars. If ever she were inclined to forget where they came from,

106

the attitude of René and Sir Stephen were there to remind her.

René, of course, had a key to O's apartment. He hadn't thought to give one to Sir Stephen, probably because, till now, Sir Stephen had not evinced the desire to visit O's place. But the fact that he had brought her home that night suddenly made René realize that this door, which only he and O could open, might be considered by Sir Stephen as an obstacle, a barrier, or as a restriction deliberately imposed by René, and that it was ridiculous to give him O if he did not at the same time give him the freedom to come and go at O's whenever he pleased. In short, he had a key made, gave it to Sir Stephen, and told O only after Sir Stephen had accepted it. She did not dream of protesting, and she soon discovered that, while she was waiting for Sir Stephen to appear, she felt incomprehensibly peaceful. She waited for a long time, wondering whether he would surprise her by coming in the middle of the night, whether he would take advantage of one of René's absences, whether he would come alone, or indeed whether he would even come at all. She did not dare speak about it to René.

One morning when the cleaning woman happened not to be there and O had gotten up earlier than usual and, at ten o'clock, was already dressed and ready to go out, she heard a key turning in the lock and flew to the door shouting: "René" (for there were times when René did arrive in this way and at this hour, and she had not dreamed it could be anyone but he). It was Sir Stephen, who smiled and said to her:

"All right, why don't we call up René."

But René, tied up at his office by a business appointment, would be there only in an hour's time.

O, her heart pounding wildly (and she wondering

why), watched Sir Stephen hang up. He sat her down on the bed, took her head in both his hands, and forced her mouth open slightly in order to kiss her. She was so out of breath that she might have slipped and fallen if he had not held her. But he did hold her, and straightened her up.

She could not understand why her throat was knotted by such a feeling of anxiety and anguish, for, after all, what did she have to fear from Sir Stephen that she had not already experienced?

He bade her remove all her clothes, and watched her, without saying a word, as she obeyed. Wasn't she, in fact, quite accustomed to being naked beneath his gaze, as she was accustomed to his silence, as she was accustomed to waiting for him to decide what his pleasure would be? She had to admit she had been deceiving herself, and that if she was taken aback by the time and the place, by the fact that she had never been naked in this room for any-one except René, the basic reason for her being upset was actually still the same: her own self-consciousness. The only difference was that this self-consciousness was made all the more apparent to her because it was not taking place in some specific spot to which she had to repair in order to submit to it, and not at night, thereby partaking of a dream or of some clandestine existence in relation to the length of the day, as Roissy had been in relation to the length of her life with René. The bright light of a May day turned the clandestine into something public: hence-forth the reality of the night and the reality of day would be one and the same. Henceforth—and O was thinking at last. This is doubtless the source of that strange senti-ment of security, mingled with terror, to which she felt she was surrendering herself and of which, without under-standing it, she had had a premonition. Henceforth there were no more hiatuses, no dead time, no remission. He

108

whom one awaits is, because he is expected, already present, already master. Sir Stephen was a far more demanding but also a far surer master than René. And however passionately O loved René, and he her, there was between them a kind of equality (were it only the equality of age) which eliminated in her any feeling of obedience, the awareness of her submission. Whatever he wanted of her she wanted too, solely because he was asking it of her. But it was as though he had instilled in her, insofar as Sir Stephen was concerned, his own admiration, his own respect. She obeyed Sir Stephen's orders as orders about which there was no question, and was grateful to him for having given them to her. Whether he addressed her in French or English, employed the familiar *tu* or the less personal *vous* form with her, she, like a stranger or a servant, never addressed him as anything but Sir Stephen. She told herself that the term "Lord" would have been more appropriate, if she had dared utter it, as he, in referring to her, would have been better advised to employ the word "slave." She also told herself that all was well, since René was happy loving in her Sir Stephen's slave.

And so, her clothes neatly arranged at the foot of the bed, having again put on her high-heeled mules, she waited, with lowered eyes, facing Sir Stephen, who was leaning against the window. Bright sunlight was streaming through the dotted muslin curtains and gently warmed her hips and thighs. She was not looking for any special effect, but it immediately occurred to her that she should have put on more perfume, she realized that she had not made up the tips of her breasts, and that, luckily, she had on her mules, for the nail polish on her toenails was beginning to peel off. Then she suddenly knew that what she was in fact waiting for in this silence, and this light, was for Sir Stephen to make some signal to her, or for him to order her to kneel down before him, unbutton him, and caress him. But no. Because she alone had been the one to whom such a thought had occurred, she turned scarlet, and as she was blushing she was thinking what a fool she was to blush: such modesty and shame in a whore!

Just then, Sir Stephen asked O to sit down before her dressing table and hear what he had to say. The dressing table was not, properly speaking, a dressing table, but next to a low ledge set into the wall, on which were arranged brushes and bottles, a large Restoration swing-mirror in which O, seated in her low-slung chair, could see herself full length.

Sir Stephen paced back and forth behind her as he talked; from time to time his reflection crossed the mirror, behind the image of O, but his was a reflection which seemed far away, because the silvering of the mirror was discolored and slightly murky.

O, her hands unclasped and her knees apart, had an urge to seize the reflection and stop it, in order to reply more easily. For Sir Stephen, speaking in a clipped English, was asking question after question, the last questions O would ever have dreamed he would ask, even assuming he would ask any in the first place. Hardly had he begun, however, when he broke off to settle O deeper and farther back in the chair; with her left leg over the arm of the chair and the other curled up slightly, O, in that bath of bright light, was then presented, to her own eyes and to Sir Stephen's, as perfectly open as though an invisible lover had withdrawn from her and left her slightly ajar.

Sir Stephen resumed his questioning, with a judgelike resolution and the skill of a father-confessor. O did not see him speaking, and saw herself replying. Whether she had, since she had returned from Roissy, belonged to other men besides René and himself? No. Whether she had wanted to belong to any other she might have met? No. Whether she caressed herself at night, when she was alone? No. Whether she had any girl friends she caressed or who she allowed to caress her? No (the "no" was more hesitant). Any girl friends she did desire? Well, there was Jacqueline, but "friend" was stretching the term. Acquaintance would be closer, or even chum, the way well-bred school girls refer to each other in high-class boarding schools.

Whereupon Sir Stephen asked her whether she had any photographs of Jacqueline, and he helped her to her feet so she could go and get them. It was in the living room that René, entering out of breath, for he had dashed up the four flights of stairs, came upon them: O was standing in front of the big table on which there shone, black and white, like puddles of water in the night, all of the pictures of Jacqueline. Sir Stephen, half-seated on the table, was taking them one by one as O handed them to him, and putting them back on the table; his other hand was holding O's womb. From that moment on, Sir Stephen, who had greeted René without letting go of her—in fact she felt his hand probe deeper into her—had ceased addressing her, and addressed himself to René. She thought she knew why: with René there, the accord between Sir Stephen and René concerning her was re-established, but apart from her, she was only the occasion for it or the object of it, they no longer had to question her, nor she to reply; what she had to do, and even what she had to be, was decided without her.

It was almost noon. The sun, falling directly on the table, curled the edges of the photographs. O wanted to move them and flatten them out to keep them from being ruined, but her fingers fumbled, she was on the verge of yielding to the burning probe of Sir Stephen's hand and allowing a moan to escape from her lips. She failed to hold it back, did in fact moan, and found herself sprawled flat on her back among the photographs, where Sir Stephen had rudely shoved her as he left her, with her legs spread and dangling. Her feet were not touching the floor; one of her mules slipped from her foot and dropped noiselessly onto the white rug. Her face was flooded with sunshine: she closed her eyes.

Later, much later, she must have remembered overhearing the conversation between Sir Stephen and René, but at the time she was not struck by it, as though it did not concern her and, simultaneously, as though she had already experienced it before. And it was true that she had already experienced a similar scene, since the first time that René had taken her to Sir Stephen's, they had discussed her in the same way. But on that initial occasion she had been a stranger to Sir Stephen, and René had done most of the talking. Since then, Sir Stephen had made her submit to all his fantasies, had molded her to his own taste, had demanded and obtained from her, as something quite routine, the most outrageous and scurrilous acts. She had nothing more to give than what he already possessed. At least so she thought.

He was speaking, he who generally was silent in her presence, and his remarks, as well as René's, revealed that they were renewing a conversation they often engaged in together, with her as the subject. It was a question of how she could best be utilized, and how the things each of them had learned from his particular use of her could best be shared. Sir Stephen readily admitted that O was infinitely more moving when her body was covered with marks, of whatever kind, if only because these marks made it impossible for her to cheat and immediately proclaimed, the moment they were seen, that anything went as far as she was concerned. For to know this was one thing, but to see the proof of it, and to see the proof constantly renewed, was quite another. René, Sir Stephen said, was perfectly right in wishing to have her whipped. They decided that she would be, irrespective of the pleasure they might derive from her screams and tears, as often as necessary so that some trace of the flogging could always be seen upon her.

O, still lying motionless on her back, her loins still aflame, was listening, and she had the feeling that by some strange substitution Sir Stephen was speaking for her, in her place. As though he was somehow in her body and could feel the anxiety, the anguish, and the shame, but also the secret pride and harrowing pleasure that she was feeling, especially when she was alone in a crowd of strangers, of passers-by in the street, or when she got into a bus, or when she was at the studio with the models and technicians, and she told herself that any and all of these people she was with, if they should have an accident and have to be laid down on the ground or if a doctor had to be called, would keep their secrets, even if they were unconscious and naked; but not she: her secret did not depend upon her silence alone, did not depend on her alone. Even if she wanted to, she could not indulge in the slightest caprice—and that was indeed the meaning of one of Sir Stephen's questions—without immediately revealing herself, she could not allow herself to partake of the most innocent acts, such as playing tennis or swimming. That these things were forbidden her was a comfort to her, a material comfort, as the bars of the convent materially prevent the cloistered girls from belonging to one another, and from escaping. For this reason too, how could she run the risk that Jacqueline would not spurn her, without at the same time running the risk of having to explain the truth to Jacqueline, or at least part of the truth?

The sun had moved and left her face. Her shoulders were sticking to the glossy surface of the photographs on which she was lying, and against her knee she could feel the rough edge of Sir Stephen's suitcoat, for he had come back beside her. He and René each took her by one hand and helped her to her feet. René picked up one of her mules. It was time for her to get dressed.

It was during the lunch that followed, at Saint-Cloud on the banks of the Seine, that Sir Stephen, who had remained alone with her, began to question her once again. The restaurant tables, covered with white tablecloths, were arranged on a shaded terrace which was bordered by privet hedges, at the foot of which was a bed of dark red, scarcely opened peonies.

Even before Sir Stephen could make a sign to her, O had obediently lifted her skirts as she sat down on the iron chair, and it had taken her bare thighs a long time to warm the cold iron. They heard the water slapping against the boats tied up to the wooden jetty at the end of the terrace. Sir Stephen was seated across from her, and O was speaking slowly, determined not to say anything that was not true. What Sir Stephen wanted to know was why she liked Jacqueline. Oh! that was easy: it was because she was too beautiful for O, like the full-sized dolls given to the poor children for Christmas, which they're afraid to touch. And yet she knew that if she had not spoken to her, and had not accosted her, it was because she really didn't want to. As she said this she raised her eyes, which had been lowered, fixed on the bed of peonies, and she realized that Sir Stephen was staring at her lips. Was he listening to what she was saying, or was he merely listening to the sound of her voice or watching the movement of

114

her lips? Suddenly she stopped speaking, and Sir Stephen's gaze rose and intercepted her own. What she read in it was so clear this time, and it was so obvious to him that she had seen it, that now it was his turn to blanch. If indeed he did love her, would he ever forgive her for having noticed it? She could neither avert her gaze nor smile, nor speak. Had her life depended on it, she would have been incapable of making a gesture, incapable of fleeing, her legs would never have carried her. He would probably never want anything from her save her submission to his desire, as long as he continued to desire her. But was desire sufficient to explain the fact that, from the day René had handed her over to him, he asked for her and kept her more and more frequently, sometimes merely to have her with him, without asking anything from her?

There he sat across from her, silent and motionless. Some businessmen, at a neighboring table, were talking as they drank a coffee so black and aromatic that the aroma was wafted all the way to their own table. Two well-groomed, contemptuous Americans lighted cigarettes halfway through their meal; the gravel crunched beneath the waiters' feet—one of them came over to refill Sir Stephen's glass, which was three-quarters empty, but what was the point of wasting good wine on a statue, a sleepwalker? The waiter did not belabor the point.

O was delighted to feel that if his gray, ardent gaze wandered from her eyes, it was to fasten on her breasts, her hands, before returning to her eyes. Finally she saw the trace of a smile appear on his lips, a smile she dared to answer. But utter a single word, impossible! She could scarcely breathe.

"O . . . ," Sir Stephen said.

"Yes," O said, faintly.

"O, what I'm going to speak to you about I have already

115

discussed with René, and we're both in accord on it. But also, I . . ." He broke off.

O never knew whether it was because, seized by a sudden chill, she had closed her eyes, or whether he too had difficulty catching his breath. He paused, the waiter was changing the plates, bringing O the menu so she could choose the dessert. O handed it to Sir Stephen. A soufflé? Yes, a soufflé. It will take twenty minutes. All right, twenty minutes. The waiter left.

"I need more than twenty minutes," Sir Stephen said.

And he went on in a steady voice, and what he said quickly convinced O that one thing at least was certain, and that was, if he did love her, nothing would be changed, unless one considered this curious respect a change, this ardor with which he was saying to her: "I'd be most pleased if you would care to . . . ," instead of simply asking her to accede to his requests. Yet they were still orders, and there was no question of O's not obeying them. She pointed this out to Sir Stephen. He admitted as much.

"I still want you to answer," he said.

"I'll do whatever you like," O responded, and the echo of what she was saying resounded in her memory: "I'll do whatever you like," she was used to saying to René, the only difference being her use of the *tu* form with René. Almost in a whisper, she murmured: "René . . ."

Sir Stephen heard it.

"René knows what I want from you. Listen to me."

He was speaking English, but in a low, carefully controlled voice which was inaudible at the neighboring tables. Whenever the waiters approached their table, he fell silent, resuming his sentence where he had left off as soon as they had moved away. What he was saying seemed strange and out of keeping with this peaceful,

116

public place, and yet what was strangest of all was that he could say it, and O hear it, so naturally.

He began by reminding her that the first evening when she had come to his apartment he had given her an order she had refused to obey, and he noted that although he might have slapped her then, he had never repeated the order since that night. Would she grant him now what she had refused him then? O understood that not only must she acquiesce, but that he wanted to hear her say it herself, in her own words, say that she would caress herself any time he asked her to. She said it, and again she saw the yellow and gray drawing room, René's departure from it, her revulsion that first evening, the fire glowing between her open knees when she was lying naked on the rug. Tonight, in this same drawing room . . . No, Sir Stephen had not specified, and was going on.

He also pointed out to her that she had never been possessed in his presence by René (or by anyone else), as she had been by him in René's presence (and at Roissy by a whole host of others). From this she should not conclude that René would be the only one to humiliate her by handing her over to a man who did not love her—and perhaps derive pleasure from it—in the presence of a man who did. (He went on at such length, and with such cruelty—she soon would open her thighs and back, and her mouth, to those of his friends who, once they had met her, might desire her—that O suspected that this coarseness was aimed as much at himself as it was at her, and the only thing she remembered was the end of the sentence: in the presence of a man who did love her. What more did she want in the way of a confession?) What was more, he would bring her back to Roissy sometime in the course of the summer. Hadn't it ever struck her as surprising, this isolation in which first René, then he, had

117

kept her? They were the only men she saw, either together, or one after the other. Whenever Sir Stephen had
invited people to his apartment on the rue de Poitiers, O
was never invited. She had never lunched or dined at his
place. Nor had René ever introduced her to any of his
friends, except for Sir Stephen. In all probability he would
continue to keep her in the background, for to Sir Stephen
was henceforth reserved the privilege of doing as he liked
with her. But she should not get the idea that she belonged to him, that she would be detained more legally;
on the contrary. (But what hurt and wounded O most was
the realization that Sir Stephen was going to treat her in
exactly the same way René had, in the same, identical
way.) The iron and gold ring that she was wearing on her
left hand—and did she recall that the ring had been
chosen so tight-fitting that they had had to force it on
her ring finger? she could not take it off—that ring was the
sign that she was a slave, but one who was common
property. It had been merely by chance that, since this
past autumn, she had not met any Roissy members who
might have noticed her irons, or revealed that they had
noticed them.

The word irons, used in the plural, which she had taken
to be an equivocal term when Sir Stephen had told her
that irons were becoming to her, had in no wise been
equivocal; it had been a mode of recognition, a password.
Sir Stephen had not had to use the second formula:
namely, whose irons was she wearing? But if today this
question were asked of O, what would she reply? O hesitated.

"René's and yours," she said.

"No," Sir Stephen said, "mine. René wants you to be
answerable first of all to me."

O was fully cognizant of this, why did she pretend she

was not? In a short while, and in any case prior to her return to Roissy, she would have to accept a definitive mark, which would not absolve her from the obligation of being a common-property slave but would, besides, reveal her to be a personal slave, Sir Stephen's, and the traces of the floggings on her body, or the marks raised by the riding crop, if indeed they were inflicted again, would be discreet and futile compared to this ultimate mark. (But what would this mark be, of what would it consist, in what way would it be definitive? O, terrified and fascinated, was dying to know, she had to know immediately. But it was obvious that Sir Stephen was not yet ready to explain it. And it was true that she had to accept, to consent in the real sense of the term, for nothing would be inflicted upon her by force to which she had not already previously consented; she could refuse, nothing was keeping her enslaved except her love and her self-enslavement. What prevented her from leaving?) And yet, before this mark was imposed upon her, even before Sir Stephen became accustomed to flogging her, as had been decided by René and himself, to flogging her in such a way that the traces were constantly visible, she would be granted a reprieve—the time required for her to make Jacqueline submit to her. Stunned, O raised her head and looked at Sir Stephen. Why? Why Jacqueline? And if Jacqueline interested Sir Stephen, why was it in relation to O?

"There are two reasons," Sir Stephen said. "The first, and least important, is that I would like to see you kiss and caress a woman."

"But even assuming she gives in to me," cried O, "how in the world do you expect me to make her consent to your being present?"

"That's the least of my worries," Sir Stephen said. "If necessary, by betrayal, and anyway I'm counting on you

119

for a great deal more than that, for the second reason why I want you to seduce her is that you're to be the bait that lures her to Roissy."

O set down the cup of coffee she was holding in her hand, shaking so violently that she spilled the viscous dregs of coffee and sugar at the bottom of the cup. Like a soothsayer, she saw unbearable images in the spreading brown stain on the tablecloth: Jacqueline's glazed eyes confronting the valet Pierre; her flanks, doubtless as golden as her breasts, though O had never seen them, exposed to view below the folds of her long red velvet dress with its tucked-up skirt; her downy cheeks stained with tears and her painted mouth open and screaming, and her straight hair, in a Dutch bob along her forehead, straight as new-mown hay—no, it was impossible, not her, not Jacqueline.

"No, it's out of the question," she said.

"Of course it's not," Sir Stephen retorted. "How do you think girls are recruited for Roissy? Once you have brought her there, the matter will be completely out of your hands, and anyway, if she wants to leave she can leave. Come along now."

He had gotten suddenly to his feet, leaving the money for the bill on the table. O followed him to the car, climbed in, and sat down. Scarcely had they entered the Bois de Boulogne when he turned in to a side road, stopped the car in a narrow lane, and took her in his arms.

III

Anne-Marie and the Rings

O had believed, or wanted to believe, in order to give herself a good excuse, that Jacqueline would be uncommonly shy. She was enlightened on this score the moment she decided to open her eyes.

The modest air Jacqueline assumed—closing the door to the mirrored make-up room where she dressed and undressed—was in fact clearly intended to inflame O, to instill in her the desire to force the door which, had it been left wide open, she would never have made up her mind to enter. That O's decision finally came from an authority outside herself, and was not the result of that basic strategy, could not have been further from Jacqueline's mind. At first O was amused by it. As she helped Jacqueline arrange her hair, for example, after Jacqueline had taken off the clothes she had posed in and was slipping into her turtle-neck sweater and the turquoise necklace the same color as her eyes, O found herself amazingly delighted at the idea that the very same evening Sir Stephen would be apprised of Jacqueline's every gesture—whether she had allowed O to fondle, through the black sweater, her small, well-spaced breasts, whether she had lowered her eyelids till those lashes, fairer than her skin,

123

were touching her cheeks; whether she had sighed or moaned. When O embraced her, she became heavy, motionless, and seemingly expectant in her arms, her lips parted slightly and her hair cascaded back. O always had to be careful to hold her by both her shoulders and lean her up against the frame of a door or against a table. Otherwise she would have slipped to the floor, her eyes closed, without a sound. The minute O let go of her, she would again turn into ice and snow, laughing and distant, and would say: "You've got lipstick on me," and would wipe her mouth. It was this distant stranger that O enjoyed betraying by carefully noting—so as not to forget anything and be able to relate everything in detail—the slow flush of her cheeks, the smell of sage and sweat. Of Jacqueline it was impossible to say that she was forbearing or that she was on her guard. When she yielded to the kisses—and all she had so far granted O were kisses, which she accepted without returning—she yielded abruptly and, it seemed, totally, as though for ten seconds, or five minutes, she had become someone else. The rest of the time she was both coquettish and coy, incredibly clever at parrying an attack, contriving never to lay herself open either to a word or gesture, or even a look which would allow the victor to coincide with the vanquished or give O to believe that it was all that simple to take possession of her mouth. The only indication one had as a guide, the only thing that gave one to suspect troubled waters beneath the calm surface of her look was an occasional, apparently involuntary trace of a smile on her triangular face, similar to the smile of a cat, as fleeting and as disturbing, and also as uncertain, as a cat's. Yet it did not take O long to realize that this smile could be provoked by two things, and Jacqueline was totally unaware of either. The first was the gifts that were given to her,

124

the second, any clear evidence of the desire she aroused—
providing, however, that the person who desired her was
someone who might be useful to her or who flattered her
vanity. In what way was O useful to her? Or was it simply
that O was an exception and that Jacqueline enjoyed being desired by O both because she took solace in O's manifest admiration and also because a woman's desire is
harmless and of no consequence? Still in all, O was convinced that if, instead of bringing Jacqueline a mother-of-
pearl brooch or the latest creation of Hermes' scarves, on
which *I Love You* was printed in every language under
the sun, she were to offer Jacqueline the hundred or two
hundred francs she seemed constantly to need, Jacqueline
would have changed her tune about never having the time
to have lunch or tea at O's place, or would have stopped
evading her caresses. But of this O never had any proof.
She had only barely mentioned it to Sir Stephen, who was
chiding her for her slowness, when René stepped in. The
five or six times that René had come by for O, when Jacqueline had happened to be there, the three of them had
gone together to the Weber bar or to one of the English
bars in the vicinity of the Madeleine; on these occasions
René would contemplate Jacqueline with precisely the
same mixture of interest, self-assurance, and arrogance
with which he would gaze, at Roissy, at the girls who
were completely at his disposal. The arrogance slid harm-
lessly off Jacqueline's solid, gleaming armor, and Jacqueline was not even aware of it. By a curious contradiction,
O was disturbed by it, judging an attitude which she considered quite natural and normal for herself, insulting
for Jacqueline. Was she taking up cudgels in defense of
Jacqueline, or was it merely that she wanted her all to
herself? She would have been hard put to answer that
question, all the more so because she did not have her all

to herself—at least not yet. But if she finally did succeed, she had to admit that it was thanks to René. On three occasions, upon leaving the bar where they had given Jacqueline considerably more whisky than she should have drunk—her cheeks were flushed and shining, her eyes hard—he had driven her home before taking O to Sir Stephen's.

Jacqueline lived in one of those lugubrious Passy lodging houses into which hordes of White Russians had piled immediately following the Revolution, and from which they had never moved. The entrance hall was painted in imitation oak, and on the stairway the spaces between the banisters were covered with dust, and the green carpeting had been worn down till it was threadbare in many places. Each time René wanted to come in—and to date he had never got beyond the front door—Jacqueline would jump out of the car, cry "not tonight" or "thanks so much," and slam the car door behind her as though she had suddenly been burned by some tongue of flame. And it was true, O would say to herself, that she was being pursued by fire. It was admirable that Jacqueline had sensed it, even though she had no concrete evidence of it as yet. At least she realized that she had to be on her guard with René, whose detachment did not seem to affect her in the slightest (or did it? and as far as seeming unaffected, two could play at that game, and René was a worthy opponent for her).

The only time that Jacqueline let O come into the house and follow her up to her room, O had understood why she had so adamantly refused René permission to set foot in the house. What would have happened to her prestige, her black-and-white legend on the slick pages of the posh fashion magazines, if someone other than a woman like herself had seen the sordid lair from which the glorious

126

creature issued forth every day? The bed was never made, at most the bedclothes were more or less pulled up, and the sheet which was visible was dirty and greasy, for Jacqueline never went to bed without massaging her face with cold cream, and she fell asleep too quickly to think of wiping it off. Sometime in the past a curtain had apparently partitioned off the toilet from the room: all that remained on the triangular shaped curtain rod were two rings and a few shreds of cloth. The color was faded from everything: from the rug, from the wallpaper whose pink and gray flowers were crawling upward like vegetation gone wild and become petrified on the imitation white trellis. One would have had to throw everything out and start again from scratch: scrape off the wallpaper, throw out the rug, sand the floors. But without waiting for that, one could in any case have cleaned off dirt that, like so many strata, ringed the enamel of the basin, immediately wiped off and put into some kind of order the bottles of make-up remover and the jars of cream, cleaned up the powder box, wiped off the dressing table, thrown out the dirty cotton, opened the windows. But, straight and cool and clean and smelling of eau de Cologne and wild flowers, dirt-proof and impeccable, Jacqueline could not have cared less about her filthy room. What she did care about, however, what caused her no end of concern, was her family.

It was because of her hovel, which O was frank enough to have mentioned to René, that René made a proposal which was to alter their lives, but it was because of her family that Jacqueline accepted. René's suggestion was that Jacqueline should come and live with O. "Family" was a gross misunderstatement: it was a clan, or rather a horde. Grandmother, mother, aunt, and even a maid—four women ranging in age from fifty to seventy, strident, heavily made up, smothered beneath their onyx and their black silks, sobbing and wailing at four in the morning in the faint red light of the icons, with the cigarette smoke swirling thickly about them, four women drowning in the clicking of tea glasses and the harsh hissing of a language Jacqueline would gladly have given half her life to forget —she was going out of her mind having to submit to their orders, to listen to them, merely having to see them. Whenever she saw her mother lifting a piece of sugar to her mouth before drinking her tea, Jacqueline would set down her own glass and retreat to her dry and dusty pigsty, leaving all three of them behind, her grandmother, her mother, and her mother's sister, with their hair dyed black, their closely knit eyebrows, and their wide, doelike, disapproving eyes—there in her mother's room which doubled as a living room, there where, besides, the fourth female, the maid, ended by resembling them. She fled, banging the doors behind her, and they called after her: "Choura, Choura, little dove," just as in the novels of Tolstoy, for her name was not Jacqueline. Jacqueline was her professional name, a name chosen to forget her real name, and with it this sordid but tender gynaeceum, and to set herself up in the French sun, in a solid world where there are men who do marry you and not disappear, as had the father she had never known, into the vast Arctic wastes from which he had never returned. She took after him completely, she used to tell herself with a mixture of anger and delight, she had his hair and high cheekbones, his complexion and his slanting eyes. All she was grateful for to her mother was having given her this blond devil as a father, this demon whom the snows had reclaimed as the earth reclaims other men. What she resented was that her mother had forgotten him quickly enough to have given birth one fine day to a dark-complexioned little girl,

the issue of a short-lived liaison, her half-sister by an unknown father, whose name was Natalie. Now fifteen, Natalie only saw them during vacation. Her father, never. But
he provided for Natalie's room and board in a *lycée* not
far from Paris, and gave her mother a monthly stipend on
which the three women and the maid—and even Jacqueline till now—had subsisted, albeit poorly, in an idleness
which to them was paradise. Whatever remained from
Jacqueline's earnings as a model, after she had bought her
cosmetics and lingerie, and her shoes and dresses—all of
which came from the top fashion houses and were, even
after the discount she received as a model, frightfully ex-
pensive—was swallowed by the gaping maw of the family
purse and disappeared, God only knows where.

Obviously, Jacqueline could have chosen to have a lover
to support her, and she had not lacked the opportunity.
She had in fact had a lover or two, less because she liked
them—not that she actually disliked them—than because
she wanted to prove to herself that she was capable of
provoking desire and inflaming a man to the point of
love. The only one of the two—the second—who had been
wealthy had made her a present of a very lovely pearl
with a slight pink tint which she wore on her left hand,
but she had refused to live with him, and since he had
refused to marry her, she had left him, with no great re-
grets, merely relieved that she was not pregnant (she had
thought she was, for several days had lived in a state of
dread at the idea). No, to live with a lover was to lose
face, to forsake one's chances for the future, it was to do
what her mother had done with Natalie's father, and that
was out of the question.

With O, however, it was quite another matter. A polite
fiction made it possible to pretend that Jacqueline was
simply moving in with a girl friend, with whom she was

going to share all costs. O would be serving a dual purpose, both playing the role of the lover who supports, or helps to support, the girl he loves, and also the theoretically opposite role of providing a moral guarantee. René's presence was not official enough, really, to compromise the fiction. But who can say whether, behind Jacqueline's decision, that very presence might not have been the real motivation for her acceptance? The fact remained that it was left up to O, and to O alone, to present the matter to Jacqueline's mother. Never had O been more keenly aware of playing the role of traitor, of spy, never had she felt so keenly she was the envoy of some criminal organization as when she found herself in the presence of that woman, who thanked her for befriending her daughter. And at the same time, deep in her heart O was repudiating her mission and the reasons which had brought her there. Yes, Jacqueline would move in with her, but never, never would O acquiesce so completely to Sir Stephen as to deliver her into his hands. And yet! . . . For no sooner had she moved into O's apartment, where she was assigned, at René's request, the bedroom he sometimes pretended to occupy (pretended, given that he always slept in O's big bed), than O, contrary to all expectations, was amazed to find herself obsessed with the burning desire to have Jacqueline at any price, even if attaining her goal meant handing her over to Sir Stephen. After all, she rationalized to herself, Jacqueline's beauty is quite sufficient protection for her, and besides, why should I get involved in it anyway? And what if she were to be reduced to what I have been reduced to, is that really so terrible?—scarcely admitting, and yet overwhelmed to imagine, how sweet it would be to see Jacqueline naked and defenseless beside her, and like her.

The week Jacqueline moved in, her mother having

given her full consent, René proved to be exceedingly zealous, inviting them every other day to dinner and taking them to the movies which, curiously enough, he chose from among the detective pictures playing, tales of drug traffic and white slavery. He would sit down between them, gently hold hands with them both, and not utter a word. But whenever there was a scene of violence, O would see him studying Jacqueline's face for the slightest trace of emotion. All you could see on it was a hint of disgust, revealed by the slight downward pout at the corners of her mouth.

Afterward he would drive them home in his convertible, with the top down, and in the open car with the windows rolled down, the speed and the night wind flattened Jacqueline's generous head of blond hair against her cheeks and narrow forehead, and even blew it into her eyes. She would toss her head to smooth her hair back into place and would run her hand through it the way boys do.

Once she had accepted the fact that she was living with O and that O was René's mistress, she consequently seemed to find René's little familiarities quite natural. It did not bother her in the least to have René come into her room under the pretense of looking for some piece of paper he had left there, and O knew that it was a pretense, for she had personally emptied the drawers of the big Dutch writing desk, with its elaborate pattern of inlay and its leather-lined leaf, which was always open, a desk so utterly unlike René. Why did he have it? Who had he gotten it from? Its weighty elegance, its light-colored woods were the only touch of wealth in the somewhat dark room which faced north and overlooked the courtyard, and the steel gray of its walls and the cold, highly waxed surface of the floor provided a sharp contrast with the cheerful rooms which faced the river. Well, there could be a virtue in that: Jacqueline would not be happy there. It would make it all the easier for her to agree to share the two front rooms with O, to sleep with O, as on the first day she had agreed to share the bathroom and kitchen, the cosmetics, the perfumes, the meals. In this, O was mistaken. Jacqueline was profoundly and passionately attached to anything that belonged to her—to her pink pearl, for instance—and completely indifferent to anything that was not hers. Had she lived in a palace, it would have interested her only if someone had told her: the palace is yours, and then proved it by giving her a notarized deed. She could not have cared less whether the gray room was pleasant or not, and it was not to get away from it that she climbed into O's bed. Nor was it to show her gratitude to O, for she in fact did not feel it, though O ascribed the feeling to her and was delighted to abuse it, or think she was abusing it. Jacqueline enjoyed pleasure, and found it both expedient and pleasant to receive it from a woman, in whose hands she was running no risks whatever.

Five days after she had unpacked her suitcases, whose contents O had helped her sort out and put away, when for the third time René had brought them home about ten o'clock after having dined with them, and had then left (as he had both other times), she simply appeared, naked and still wet from her bath, in O's doorway and said to O:

"You're sure he's not coming back?" and without even waiting for her answer, she slipped into the big bed. She allowed herself to be kissed and caressed, her eyes closed, not responding by a single caress; at first she moaned faintly, hardly more than a whimper, then louder, still louder, until finally she cried out. She fell asleep sprawled across the bed, her knees apart but her legs flat again on the bed, the upper part of her body slightly turned on one side, her hands open, her body bathed in the bright light of the pink lamp. Between her breasts a trace of sweat glistened. O covered her and turned out the light. When, two hours later, she took her again, in the dark, Jacqueline did not resist, but murmured:

"Don't wear me out completely, I have to get up early tomorrow."

It was at this same time that Jacqueline, in addition to her intermittent assignments as a model, began to engage in a more absorbing but equally unpredictable career: she was signed up to play bit parts in the movies. It was hard to tell whether she was proud of this or not, whether or not she considered this the first step in a career which might lead to her becoming famous. In the morning she would drag herself out of bed more in anger than with any show of enthusiasm, would take her shower, quickly make herself up, for breakfast would accept only the large cup of black coffee that O barely had time to make for her, and would let O kiss the tips of her fingers, responding with no more than a mechanical smile and an expression full of malice: O was soft and warm in her white vicuña dressing gown, her hair combed, her face washed, looking for all the world like someone who plans on going back to bed. And yet such was not the case. O had not yet found the courage to explain why to Jacqueline. The truth of the matter was that every day, when Jacqueline left for the film studio at Boulogne where her picture was being shot, at the same time as the children left for school and the white-collar workers for their offices, O, who in the past had indeed whiled away the morning in her apartment, also got dressed.

"I'm sending you my car," Sir Stephen had said, "to

drive Jacqueline to Boulogne, then it will come back to pick you up."

Thus O found herself headed for Sir Stephen's place every morning when the sun along the way was still striking the eastern façades; the other walls were still cool in the shade, but in the gardens the shadows were already growing shorter.

At the rue de Poitiers, the housework was still not finished. Norah, the mulatto maid, would take O into the small bedroom where, the first evening, Sir Stephen had left her alone to sleep and cry, wait till O had put her gloves, her bag, and her clothes on the bed, and then she would take them and put them away, in O's presence, in a closet to which she alone had the key. Then, having given O the patent-leather high-heeled mules which made a sharp clicking sound as she walked, Norah would precede her, opening the doors as they went, till they reached Sir Stephen's study, when she would stand aside to let O pass.

O never got used to these preparations, and stripping in front of this patient old woman, who never said a word to her and scarcely looked at her, seemed to her as dangerous and formidable as being naked at Roissy in the presence of the valets there. On felt slippers, the old lady slipped silently by like a nun. As she followed her, O could not take her eyes off the twin points of her Madras kerchief and, every time she opened a door, off her thin, swarthy hand on the porcelain handle, a hand that seemed as hard as wood.

At the same time, by a feeling diametrically opposed to the terror she inspired in her—a contradiction O was unable to explain—O experienced a kind of pride that this servant of Sir Stephen (and just what was her relation to Sir Stephen, and why had he entrusted her with this task as costume and make-up assistant for which she seemed so poorly suited?) was a witness to the fact that she too—like so many others, perhaps, whom she had guided in the same way, and why should she think otherwise?—was worthy of being used by Sir Stephen. For perhaps Sir Stephen did love her, without a doubt he did, and O sensed that the time was not far off when he would no longer be content to let her suspect it but would declare it to her—but to the very degree that his love and desire for her were increasing, he was becoming more completely, more minutely, and more deliberately exacting with her. Thus retained by his side for whole mornings, during which he sometimes scarcely touched her, wanting only to be caressed by her, she did whatever he wanted of her with a sentiment that must be qualified as gratitude, which was all the greater whenever his request took the form of a command. Each surrender was for her the pledge that another surrender would be demanded of her, and she acquitted herself of each as though of a duty performed; it was odd that she should have been completely satisfied by it, and yet she was.

Sir Stephen's office, situated directly above the yellow and gray drawing room where he held sway in the evening, was smaller and had a lower ceiling. It contained neither settee nor sofa, only two Regency armchairs upholstered in a tapestry with a floral pattern. O sat in one occasionally, but Sir Stephen generally preferred to keep her near at hand, at arm's length, and while he was busy with other things, to none the less have her seated on his desk, to his left. The desk was set at right angles to the wall, which allowed O to lean back against the shelves which contained some dictionaries and leather-bound phone books. The telephone was snug against her left thigh, and every time the phone rang she jumped. It was she who picked up the receiver and answered, saying:

"May I ask who's calling?" then either repeating the name out loud and passing the receiver to Sir Stephen, or, if he signaled to her, making some excuse for him. Whenever he had a visitor, old Norah would announce him, Sir Stephen would have him wait long enough for Norah to conduct O back to the room where she had undressed and where, after Sir Stephen's visitor had left, she would come to fetch her again when Sir Stephen rang for her.

Since Norah entered and left the study several times each morning, either to bring Sir Stephen his coffee or to bring in the mail, to open or draw the blinds or to empty the ash trays, and since she alone had the right to enter and had been expressly instructed never to knock, and since, finally, she always waited in silence whenever she had something to say, until Sir Stephen spoke to her to ask her what it was she wanted, it so happened that on one occasion when Norah came into the room O was bent over the desk with her rear exposed, her head and arms against the leather top, waiting for Sir Stephen to impale her. She raised her head. If Norah had not glanced at her, and she invariably never did, that would have been the only movement O would have made. But this time it was obvious that Norah was trying to catch O's eye. Those black, beady eyes fastened on her own—and it was impossible for O to tell whether they bespoke indifference or not—those eyes set in a deeply furrowed, impassive face so bothered O that she made a movement to try and get away from Sir Stephen. He gathered what it was all about, and with one hand pinned her waist to the table, while prying her open with the other. She who was constantly striving to cooperate and do her best was now, quite involuntarily, tense and contracted, and Sir Stephen was obliged to force his way. Even when he had done so, she felt that the ring of her buttocks was tightening around

136

him, and he had trouble forcing himself all the way into her. He withdrew only when he was certain he could come and go with ease. Then, as he was on the point of taking her again, he told Norah to wait, and said that she could help O get dressed when he had finished with her. And yet, before he dismissed her, he kissed O tenderly on the mouth. It was that kiss which, several days later, gave her the courage to tell him that Norah frightened her.

"I should hope so," he retorted. "And when you wear my mark and my irons, as I trust you soon will—if you will consent to it—you'll have much more reason to be afraid of her."

"Why?" O asked, "and what mark and what irons? I'm already wearing this ring...."

"That's completely up to Anne-Marie, to whom in fact I've promised to show you. We're going to pay her a visit after lunch. I trust you don't mind? She's a friend of mine, and you may have noted that, till now, I've refrained from ever introducing you to my friends. When Anne-Marie is finished with you, I'll give you genuine reasons for being afraid of Norah."

O did not dare to pursue the matter any further. This Anne-Marie whom they had threatened her with intrigued her more than Norah. Sir Stephen had already mentioned her when they had lunched together at Saint-Cloud. And it was quite true that O knew none of Sir Stephen's friends, nor any of his acquaintances. In short, she was living in Paris locked in her secret as though she had been locked in a brothel; the only persons who had the key to her secret, René and Sir Stephen, at the same time had the only key to her body. She could not help thinking that the expression "open oneself to someone," which meant to give oneself, for her had only one meaning, a literal, physical, and in fact absolute meaning, for she was in fact

137

opening every part of her body which was capable of being opened. It also seemed to her that this was her *raison d'être* and that Sir Stephen, like René, intended it should be, since whenever he spoke of his friends as he had done at Saint-Cloud, it was to tell her that those to whom he might introduce her would, needless to say, be free to dispose of her however they wished, if indeed they did. But in trying to visualize Anne-Marie and imagine what it might be that Sir Stephen expected from Anne-Marie as far as she, O, was concerned, O was completely at sea, and not even her experience at Roissy was of any help to her. Sir Stephen had also mentioned that he wanted to see her caress another woman; could that be it? (But he had specified that he was referring to Jacqueline. . . .) No, it wasn't that. "To show you," he had just said. Indeed. But after she left Anne-Marie, O knew no more than before.

Anne-Marie lived not far from the Observatoire in Paris, in an apartment flanked by a kind of large studio, on the top floor of a new building overlooking the treetops. She was a slender woman, the same age more or less as Sir Stephen, and her black hair was streaked with gray. Her eyes were such a deep blue they looked black. She offered O and Sir Stephen some coffee, a very strong, bitter coffee which she served steaming hot in tiny cups, and which reassured O. When she had finished her coffee and got up from her chair to put down her empty cup on a coffee table, Anne-Marie seized her by the wrist and, turning to Sir Stephen, said:

"May I?"

"Please do," Sir Stephen said.

Then Anne-Marie, who till then had neither spoken to

nor smiled at O, even to greet her or to acknowledge Sir Stephen's introduction, said to her softly, with a smile so tender one would have thought she were giving her a present:

"Come, my child, and let me see your belly and back-side. But better yet, why don't you take off all your clothes."

While O obeyed, she lighted a cigarette. Sir Stephen had not taken his eyes off O. They left her standing there for perhaps five minutes. There was no mirror in the room, but O caught a vague reflection of herself in the black lacquer surface of a screen.

"Take off your stockings too," Anne-Marie said suddenly. "You see," she went on, "you shouldn't wear garters, you'll ruin your thighs." And with the tip of her finger she pointed to the spot just above O's knees where O rolled down her stockings around a wide elastic garter. There was in fact a faint mark on her leg.

"Who told you to do that?"

Before O had a chance to reply, Sir Stephen said:

"The boy who gave her to me, you know him, René." And he added: "But I'm sure he'll come around to your opinion."

"I'm glad to hear it," said Anne-Marie. "I'm going to give you some long, dark stockings, O, and a corset to hold them up. But it will be a whalebone corset, one that will be snug at the waist."

When Anne-Marie had rung and a young, blond, silent girl had brought in some very sheer, black stockings and a tight-fitting corset of black nylon taffeta, reinforced and sustained by wide, close-set stays which curved in at the lower belly and above the hips. O, who was still standing, shifting her weight from one foot to the other, slipped on the stockings, which came to the top of her thighs. The

139

young blonde helped her into the corset, which had a row of buckles along one of the busks on one side near the back. Like the bodices at Roissy, this one could be laced up as tightly or loosely as desired, the laces being at the back. O fastened her stockings to the four garter-belt snaps in front and on the sides, then the girl set about lacing her up as tight as she could. O felt her waist and belly being pressed inward by the pressure of the stays, that in front descended almost to the pubis, which they left free, as they did her hips. The corset was shorter behind and left her rear completely free.

"She'll be much improved," Anne-Marie said, speaking to Sir Stephen, "when her waist is a fraction of its present size. And what's more, if you're too pressed for time to have her undress, you'll see that the corset is no inconvenience. Now then, O, step over this way."

The girl left, O went over to Anne-Marie, who was sitting in a low chair, a small easy chair upholstered in bright red velvet. Anne-Marie ran her hand lightly over her buttocks and then, toppling her over an ottoman similar to the red velvet chair and ordering her not to move, seized both her nether lips.

This is how they lift the fish at the market, O was thinking, by the gills, and how they pry open the mouths of horses. She also recalled that the valet Pierre, during her first evening at Roissy, had done the same to her after having fastened her in chains. After all, she was no longer mistress of her own fate, and that part of her of which she was least in control was most assuredly that half of her body which could, so to speak, be put to use independently of the rest. Why, each time that she realized this, was she—surprised was not really the right word—once again persuaded, why was she paralyzed each time by the same feeling of profound distress, a sentiment which tended to deliver her not so much into the hands of the person she was with as into the hands of him who had turned her over to alien hands, a sentiment which drew her closer to René when others were possessing her and which, here, was tending to draw her closer to whom? To René or to Sir Stephen? She no longer knew. . . . But that was because she did not want to know, for it was clear that she had belonged to Sir Stephen now for . . . how long had it been? . . .

Anne-Marie had her stand up and put her clothes back on.

"You can bring her to me whenever you like," she said to Sir Stephen. "I'll be at Samois (Samois . . . O had expected: Roissy. But it did not mean Roissy; then what did it mean?) in two days' time. That will be fine." (What would be fine?)

"In ten days, if that suits you," Sir Stephen said, "at the beginning of July."

In the car which was driving her back home, Sir Stephen having remained behind at Anne-Marie's, she remembered the statue she had seen as a child in the Luxembourg Gardens: a woman whose waist had been similarly constricted and seemed so slim between her full breasts and plump behind—she was leaning over limpid waters, a spring which, like her, was carefully sculptured in marble, looking at her reflection—so slim and frail that she had been afraid the marble waist would snap. But if that was what Sir Stephen wanted . . .

As for Jacqueline, she could handle her easily enough merely by telling her the corset was one of René's whims. Which brought O back to a train of thought she had been trying to avoid whenever it occurred to her, one which surprised her above all not to find more painful: why, since Jacqueline had moved in with her, had he made an effort not so much to leave her alone with Jacqueline, which she could understand, but to avoid being alone with O any more? July was fast approaching, and he would be going away and would not be coming to visit her at this Anne-Marie's where Sir Stephen was sending her; must she therefore resign herself to the fact that the only times she would see him would be those evenings when he was in the mood to invite Jacqueline and her, or—and she didn't know which of the two possibilities upset her most (since between them, at this point, there was something basically false, due to the fact that their relationship was so circumscribed)—on those occasional mornings when she was at Sir Stephen's and Norah ushered René in, after first having announced his arrival? Sir Stephen always received him, invariably René kissed O, caressed the tips of her breasts, coordinated his plans with Sir Stephen for the following day—plans which never included O—and left. Had he given her to Sir Stephen so completely that he had ceased to love her? The thought threw O into such a state of panic that, mechanically, she got out of Sir Stephen's car in front of her house, instead of telling the chauffeur to wait, and after it had pulled away she had to dash off in search of a taxi. Taxis are few and far between on the quai de Bethune. O had to run all the way to the boulevard Saint-Germain, and still she had to wait. She was all out of breath and in a sweat, because her corset made it hard for her to breathe, when a taxi finally slowed down at the corner of the rue Cardinal-Lemoine. She signaled to it, gave the driver the address of René's office, got in without knowing whether René would be there, and, if he was, whether he would see her; it was the first time she had gone to his office.

She was not surprised by the impressive building on a

142

side street just off the Champs-Elysées, or by the American-style offices, but what did disconcert her was René's attitude, although he did receive her immediately. Not that he was aggressive or full of reproaches. She would have preferred reproaches, for he had never given her permission to come and disturb him at his office, and it was possible that she was creating a considerable disturbance for him. He dismissed his secretary, told her that he did not want to see anyone, and asked her to hold all calls. Then he asked O what was the matter.

"I was afraid you didn't love me any longer," O said.

He laughed. "All of a sudden, just like that?"

"Yes, in the car coming back from ..."

"Coming back from where?"

O remained silent.

René laughed again:

"But I know where you were, silly. Coming back from Anne-Marie's. And in ten days you're going to Samois. Sir Stephen just talked to me on the phone."

René was seated in the only comfortable chair in the office, which was facing the table, and O had buried herself in his arms.

"They can do whatever they want with me, I don't care," she murmured. "But tell me you still love me."

"Of course I love you, darling," René said, "but I want you to obey me, and I'm afraid you're not doing a very good job of it. Did you tell Jacqueline that you belonged to Sir Stephen, did you talk to her about Roissy?"

O assured him that she had not. Jacqueline acquiesced to her caresses, but the day she should learn that O ...

René stopped her from completing her sentence, lifted her up and laid her down in the chair where he had just been sitting, and bunched up her skirt.

"Ah ha, so you have your corset," he said. "It's true that

143

you'll be much more attractive when you have a smaller waistline."

Then he took her, and it seemed to O that it had been so long since he had that, subconsciously, she realized she had begun to doubt whether he really desired her any longer, and in his act she saw a proof of love.

"You know," he said afterward, "you're foolish not to talk to Jacqueline. We absolutely need her at Roissy, and the simplest way of getting her there would be through you. Besides, when you come back from Anne-Marie's there won't be any way of concealing your true condition any longer."

O wanted to know why.

"You'll see," René went on. "You still have five days, and only five days, because Sir Stephen intends to start whipping you again daily, five days before he sends you to Anne-Marie's, and there will be no way for you to hide the marks. How will you ever explain them to Jacqueline?"

O did not reply. What René did not know was that Jacqueline was completely egotistical as far as O was concerned, being interested in her solely because of O's manifest, and passionate, interest in her, and she never looked at O. If O were covered with welts from the floggings, all she would have to do would be to take care not to bathe in Jacqueline's presence, and to wear a nightgown. Jacqueline would never notice a thing. She had never noticed that O did not wear panties, and there was no danger she would notice anything else: the fact was that O did not interest her.

"Listen to me," René went on, "there's one thing anyway I want you to tell her, and tell her right away, and that is that I'm in love with her."

"Is that true?" O said.

"I want her," René said, "and since you can't—or won't

144

—do anything about it, I'll take charge of the matter myself and do what has to be done."

"You'll never get her to agree to go to Roissy," O said.

"I won't? In that case," René retorted, "we'll force her to."

That night, after dark, when Jacqueline was in bed and O had pulled the covers back to gaze at her in the light of the lamp, after having said to her: "René's in love with you, you know"—for she had delivered the message and delivered it without delay—O, who a month before had been horrified at the idea of seeing this delicate wisp of a body scored by the lash, these narrow loins quartered, the pure mouth screaming, and the fair down on her cheeks streaked with tears, O now repeated to herself René's final words, and was happy.

With Jacqueline gone and not due back until the beginning of August, if they had finished shooting the film she was making, there was nothing further to keep O in Paris. July was around the corner, all the gardens in Paris were bursting with crimson geraniums, at noon all the shutters in town were closed, and René was complaining that he would have to make a trip to Scotland. For a moment O was hoping that he would take her along. But apart from the fact that he never took her anywhere to see his family, she knew that he would surrender her to Sir Stephen, if he were to ask for her.

Sir Stephen announced that he would come for her the same day that René was flying to London. She was on vacation.

"We're going down to Anne-Marie's," he said, "she's expecting you. Don't bother packing a suitcase, you won't need anything."

Their destination was not the apartment near the Observatoire where O had first met Anne-Marie, but a low-lying two-story house at the end of a large garden, on the edge of the Fontainebleau Forest. Since that first day, O had been wearing the whalebone corset that Anne-Marie had deemed so essential: each day she had tightened it a little more, until now her waist was scarcely larger than the circle formed by her ten fingers; Anne-Marie ought to be pleased.

When they arrived it was two o'clock in the afternoon, the whole house was asleep, and the dog barked faintly when they rang the bell: a big, shaggy, sheepdog that sniffed at O's knees beneath her skirt. Anne-Marie was sitting under a copper beech tree on the edge of the lawn which, in one corner of the garden, faced the windows of her bedroom. She did not get up.

"Here's O," Sir Stephen said. "You know what has to be done with her. When will she be ready?"

Anne-Marie glanced at O. "You mean you haven't told her? All right, I'll begin immediately. You should probably allow ten days after it's over. I imagine you'll want to put the rings and monogram on yourself? Come back in two weeks. The whole business should be finished two weeks after that."

O started to ask a question.

"Just a minute, O," Anne-Marie said, "go into the front bedroom over there, get undressed but keep your sandals on, and come back."

The room, a large white bedroom with heavy purple Jouy print drapes, was empty. O put her bag, her gloves, and her clothes on a small chair near a closet door. There was no mirror. She went back outside and, dazzled by the bright sunlight, walked slowly back over to the shade of the beech tree. Sir Stephen was still standing in front of

146

Anne-Marie, the dog at his feet. Anne-Marie's black hair, streaked with gray, shone as though she had used some kind of cream on it, her blue eyes seemed black. She was dressed in white, with a patent-leather belt around her waist, and she was wearing patent-leather sandals which revealed the bright red nail polish on the toenails of her bare feet, the same color polish she was wearing on her fingernails.

"O," she said, "kneel down in front of Sir Stephen."

O obliged, her arms crossed behind her back, the tips of her breasts quivering. The dog tensed, as though he were about to spring at her.

"Down, Turk," Anne-Marie ordered. Then: "Do you consent, O, to bear the rings and the monogram with which Sir Stephen desires you to be marked, without knowing how they will be placed upon you?"

"I do," O said.

"All right then, I'm going to walk Sir Stephen to his car. Stay here."

As Anne-Marie got up from her chaise longue, Sir Stephen bent down and took O's breasts in his hands. He kissed her on the mouth and murmured:

"Are you mine, O, are you really mine?" then turned and left her, to follow Anne-Marie. The gate banged shut, Anne-Marie was coming back. O, her legs folded beneath her, was sitting on her heels and had her arms on her knees, like an Egyptian statue.

There were three other girls living in the house, all of whom had a bedroom on the second floor. O was given a small bedroom on the ground floor, adjoining Anne-Marie's. Anne-Marie called up to them to come down into the garden. Like O, all three of them were naked. The only persons in this gynaeceum—which was carefully concealed by the high walls and by closed shutters over the

147

windows which overlooked a narrow dirt road—the only persons who wore clothes were Anne-Marie and the three servants: a cook and two maids, all of whom were older than Anne-Marie, three severe, dour women in their black alpaca skirts and stiffly starched aprons.

"Her name is O," said Anne-Marie, who had sat down again. "Bring her over to me so I can get a better look at her. Two of the girls helped O to her feet: they were both brunettes, their hair as dark as their fleece below, and the nipples of their breasts were large and dark, almost purple. The other girl was a short, plump redhead, and the chalky skin of her bosom was crisscrossed by a terrifying network of green veins. The two girls pushed O till she was right next to Anne-Marie, who pointed to the three black stripes that showed on the front of her thighs and were repeated on her buttocks.

"Who whipped you?" she asked. "Sir Stephen?"

"Yes," O said.

"When? and with what?"

"Three days ago, with a riding crop."

"Starting tomorrow, and for a month thereafter, you will not be whipped. But today you will, to mark your arrival, as soon as I've had a chance to examine you. Has Sir Stephen ever whipped you on the inside of your thighs, with you legs spread wide? No? It's true, men don't know how to. Well, we'll soon see. Show me your waist. Yes, it's much better!"

Anne-Marie pressed O's waist to make it even more wasplike. Then she sent the redhead to fetch another corset and had them put it on her. It was also made of black nylon, but was so stiffly whaleboned and so narrow that it looked for all the world like an extremely wide belt. It had no garter straps. One of the girls laced it up as tight as she could, with Anne-Marie lending her encouragement as she pulled on the laces as hard as she could.

"This is dreadful," O said. "I don't know whether I can bear it."

"That's the whole point," Anne-Marie said. "You're much much lovelier than you were, but the problem was you didn't lace it tight enough. You're going to wear it this way every day. But tell me now, how did Sir Stephen prefer using you? I need to know."

She had seized O's womb with her whole hand, and O could not reply. Two of the girls were seated on the lawn, the third, one of the brunettes, was seated on the foot of Anne-Marie's chaise longue.

"Turn her around for me, girls, so I can see her back," Anne-Marie said.

She was turned around and bent over, and the hands of both girls vented her.

"Of course," Anne-Marie went on, "there was no need for you to tell me. You'll have to be marked on the rear. Stand up. We're going to put on your bracelets. Colette, go get the box, we'll draw lots to see who will whip you. Bring the tokens, Colette, then we'll go to the music room."

Colette was the taller of the two dark-haired girls, the other's name was Claire; the short redhead was named Yvonne. O had not noticed till now that they were all wearing, as at Roissy, a leather collar and leather bracelets on their wrists. They were also wearing similar bracelets around their ankles.

When Yvonne had chosen some bracelets that fit O and put them on her, Anne-Marie handed O four tokens and asked her to give one to each of the girls, without looking at the numbers on them. O handed out the tokens. The

149

three girls each looked at theirs but said nothing, waiting for Anne-Marie to speak.

"I have number two," Anne-Marie said. "Who has number one?"

Colette had number one.

"All right, take O away, she's all yours."

Colette seized O's arms and joined her hands behind her back; she fastened the bracelets together and pushed O ahead of her. On the threshold of a French door that opened into a small wing which formed an L with the front of the house, Yvonne, who was leading the way, removed her sandals. The light entering through the French door revealed a room the far end of which formed a kind of raised rotunda; the ceiling, in the shape of a shallow cupola, was supported by two narrow columns set about six feet apart. This dais was about four steps high and, in the area between the columns, projected further into the room in a gentle arc. The floor of the rotunda, like that of the rest of the room, was covered with a red felt carpet. The walls were white, the curtains on the windows red, and the sofas set in a semicircle facing the rotunda were upholstered in the same red felt material as the carpet on the floor. In the rectangular portion of the room there was a fireplace which was wider than it was deep, and opposite the fireplace a large console-type combination record player and radio, with shelves of records on both sides. This was why it was called the music room, which communicated directly with Anne-Marie's bedroom via a door near the fireplace. The identical door on the other side of the fireplace opened into a closet. Aside from the record player and the sofas, the room had no furniture.

While Colette had O sit down on the edge of the platform, which in this center portion between the columns made a vertical drop to the floor—the steps having been placed to the left and right of the columns—the two other girls, after first having closed the Venetian blinds a trifle, shut the French door. O was surprised to note that it was a double door, and Anne-Marie, who was laughing, said:

"That's so no one can hear you scream. And the walls are lined with cork. Don't worry, no one can hear the slightest thing that goes on in here. Now lie down."

She took her by both shoulders and laid her back, then pulled her slightly forward. O's hands were clutching the edge of the platform—Yvonne having attached them to a ring set in the platform—and her buttocks were thus suspended in mid-air. Anne-Marie made her raise her legs toward her chest, then O suddenly felt her legs, still doubled-up above her, being pulled taut in the same direction: straps had been fastened to her ankle bracelets and thence to the columns on either side, while she lay thus between them on this raised dais exposed in such a way that the only part of her which was visible was the double cleft of her womb and her buttocks violently quartered. Anne-Marie caressed the inside of her thighs.

"It's the most tender spot of the whole body," she said, "be careful not to harm it. Not too hard now, Colette."

Colette was standing over her, astride her at the level of her waist, and in the bridge formed by her dark legs O could see the tassles of the whip she was holding in her hand. As the first blows burned into her loins, O moaned. Colette alternated from left to right, paused, then started again. O struggled with all her might, she thought the straps would tear her limb from limb. She did not want to grovel, she did not want to beg for mercy. And yet that was precisely what Anne-Marie intended wringing from her lips.

"Faster," she said to Colette, "and harder."

O braced herself, but it was no use. A minute later she could bear it no more, she screamed and burst into tears, while Anne-Marie caressed her face.

"Just a second longer," she said, "and it will be over. Only five more minutes. She can scream for five minutes. It's twenty-five past, Colette. Stop when it's half past, when I tell you to."

But O was screaming:

"No, no, for God's sake don't!" screaming that she couldn't bear it, no, she couldn't bear the torture another second. And yet she endured it to the bitter end, and after Colette had left the little stage, Anne-Marie smiled at her.

"Thank me," she said to O, and O thanked her.

She knew very well why Anne-Marie had wanted, above all else, to have her whipped. That the female of the species was as cruel as, and more implacable than, the male, O had never doubted for a minute. But O suspected that Anne-Marie was less interested in making a spectacle of her power than she was in establishing between O and herself a sense of complicity. O had never really understood, but she had finally come to accept as an undeniable and important verity, this constant and contradictory jumble of her emotions: she liked the idea of torture, but when she was being tortured herself she would have betrayed the whole world to escape it, and yet when it was over she was happy to have gone through it, happier still if it had been especially cruel and prolonged. Anne-Marie had been correct in her assumptions both as to O's acquiescence and as to her revolt, and knew that her pleas for mercy were indeed genuine. There was still a third reason for what she had done, which she explained to O. She was bent on proving to every girl who came into her house, and who was fated to live in a totally feminine universe, that her condition as a woman should not be minimized or

152

denigrated by the fact that she was in contact only with other women, but that, on the contrary, it should be heightened and intensified. That was why she required that the girls be constantly naked; the way in which O was flogged, as well as the position in which she was bound, had no other purpose. Today it was O who would remain for the rest of the afternoon—for three more hours—exposed on the dais, her legs raised and spread. Tomorrow it would be Claire, or Colette, or Yvonne, whom O would contemplate in turn. It was a technique much too slow and meticulous (as was the way the whip was wielded) to be used at Roissy. But O would see how efficient it was. Apart from the rings and the letters she would wear when she left, she would be returned to Sir Stephen more open, and more profoundly enslaved, than she had ever before thought was possible.

The following morning, after breakfast, Anne-Marie told O and Yvonne to follow her into her bedroom. From her writing desk she took a green leather coffer which she set on the bed and proceeded to open. Both girls squatted on their heels.

"Hasn't Yvonne said anything to you about this?" Anne-Marie asked O.

O shook her head. What was there for Yvonne to tell her?

"And I know Sir Stephen didn't either. No matter. Anyway, here are the rings he wants you to wear."

The rings were of stainless steel, unburnished, the same dull finish as the gold-plated iron ring. They were oblong in shape, similar to the links of a heavy chain, the rounded metal being approximately as thick as the diameter of an oversized coloring pencil. Anne-Marie showed O that each ring was composed of two U-shaped halves, one of which fitted into the other.

"This is only the test model," she said, "which can be removed after it's been inserted. The permanent model, you see, has a spring inside, and when you press on it it locks into the female slot of the other half of the ring and cannot be removed, except by filing."

Each ring was as long as two joints of the little finger and wide enough for the same little finger to slip through .it. To each ring was suspended, like another ring, or as though to the supporting loop of an earring, a ring which was meant to hang parallel to the plane of the ear and form its extension, a round disk made of the same metal, whose diameter was the same size as the ring was long. On one of its faces, a triskelion in gold inlay; on the opposite face, nothing.

"On the blank side will be your name, your title, and Sir Stephen's family and given names," Anne-Marie said, "with, below it, a design composed of a crossed whip and riding crop. Yvonne is wearing a disk just like it on her necklace, but yours will be worn on your loins."

"But . . . ," O ventured.

"I know," Anne-Marie replied, "that's why I brought Yvonne along. Show yours, Yvonne."

The red-haired girl rose to her feet and lay back on the bed. Anne-Marie spread her thighs and showed O that one of the nether lobes had been neatly pierced, half way down and close to the base. The iron ring would just fit into it.

"In a moment I'll pierce you, O," Anne-Marie said. "It's nothing really. What takes the longest is placing the clamps so as to be able to suture the outer and inner layers, attach the epidermis to the inner membrane. It's much easier to bear than the whip."

"You mean to say you won't put me to sleep?" O cried, trembling.

"Of course not," Anne-Marie replied. "You'll merely be tied a little more tightly than you were yesterday. That's really quite sufficient. Now come along."

A week later Anne-Marie removed the clamps and slipped on the test ring. It was lighter than it looked, for it was hollow, but still O could feel its weight. The hard metal, which was visibly piercing the flesh, looked like an instrument of torture. What would it be like when the weight of the second ring was added to it? This barbaric instrument would be immediately and glaringly apparent to the most casual glance.

"Of course it will," Anne-Marie said, when O pointed this out to her. "But aren't you by now fully aware of what Sir Stephen wants? Anyone, at Roissy or anywhere else, Sir Stephen or anyone else, even you in front of the mirror, anyone who lifts your skirts will immediately see his rings on your loins and, if you turn around, his monogram on your buttocks. You may possibly file the rings off one day, but the brand on your backside will never come off."

"I thought it was possible to have tattoos removed," Colette said. (It was she who had tattoed, on Yvonne's white skin just above the triangle of her belly, the initials of Yvonne's master in ornate blue letters, like the letters you find on embroidery.)

"O will not be tattoed," replied Anne-Marie.

O looked at Anne-Marie. Colette and Yvonne were stunned, and said nothing. Anne-Marie was fumbling for her words.

"Go ahead and say it," O said.

"My poor dear girl, I just couldn't work up the courage to tell you: you're to be branded. Sir Stephen sent me the branding irons two days ago."

"Branded?" Yvonne cried, "with a red-hot branding iron?"

From the first day, O had shared in the life of the house. Idleness, absolute and deliberate idleness was the order of the day, interspersed with dull distractions. The girls were at liberty to walk in the garden, to read, draw, play cards, play solitaire. They could sleep in their rooms or sunbathe on the lawn. Sometimes two of them would chat, or they would talk together in pairs for hours on end, and sometimes they would sit at Anne-Marie's feet without uttering a word. Mealtimes were always the same, dinner was by candlelight, tea was served in the garden, and there was something absurd about the matter-of-fact way in which the two servants served these naked girls seated around a festive table.

In the evening, Anne-Marie would designate one of them to sleep with her, sometimes the same one several nights in succession. She caressed her chosen partner and was by her caressed, generally toward dawn, and then she would immediately fall asleep, after having sent her partner back to her own room. The purple drapes, only half closed, tinted the dawning day mauve, and Yvonne used to say that Anne-Marie was as beautiful and haughty in receiving pleasure as she was unstinting in her demands. None of them had ever seen her naked. She would pull up or open slightly her white nylon nightgown, but would not take it off. Neither the pleasure she may have tasted the night before nor her choice of partner the previous evening had the least influence on her decision the following afternoon, which was always determined by a drawing. At three in the afternoon, beneath the copper beech where the garden chairs were grouped about a round, white-marble table, Anne-Marie would bring out the token box. Each girl would take a token. Whoever drew the lowest number was then taken to the music room and arranged on the dais as O had been that first day. She then had to point to (save for O, who was exempted until her departure) Anne-Marie's right or left hand, in each of which she was holding a white or black ball. If she chose black, she was flogged; white, she was not. Anne-Marie never resorted to chicanery, even if chance condemned or spared the same girl several days in a row. Thus the torture of little Yvonne, who sobbed and cried out for her lover, was repeated four days running. Her thighs, like her breasts crisscrossed with a green network of veins, spread to reveal a pink flesh which was pierced by the thick iron ring, which had finally been inserted, and the spectacle was all the more striking because Yvonne was completely shaved.

"But why?" O wanted to know, "and why the ring if you are already wearing a disk on your collar?"

"He says I'm more naked when I'm shaved. The ring, I think the ring is to fasten me with."

Yvonne's green eyes and her tiny triangular face reminded O of Jacqueline every time she looked at her. What if Jacqueline were to go to Roissy? Sooner or later, Jacqueline would end up here, would here be strapped on her back on this platform.

"I won't," O would say, "I don't want to and I won't lift a finger to get her there. As it is, I've already said too much. Jacqueline's not the sort to be flogged and marked."

But how admirably suited to blows and irons was little Yvonne, how lovely it was to hear her moans and sighs, how lovely too to witness her body soaked with perspiration, and what a pleasure to wrest the moans and the sweat from her. For on two occasions Anne-Marie had handed O the thonged whip—both times the victim had been Yvonne—and told her to use it. The first time, for the first minute, she had hesitated, and at Yvonne's first scream O had recoiled and cringed, but as soon as she had started in again and Yvonne's cries had echoed anew, she had been overwhelmed with a terrible feeling of pleasure, a feeling so intense that she had caught herself laughing in spite of herself, and she had found it almost impossible to restrain herself from striking Yvonne as hard as she could. Afterward she had remained next to Yvonne throughout the entire period of time she was kept tied up, embracing her from time to time. In some ways, she probably resembled Yvonne. At least one was led to suspect as much by the way Anne-Marie felt about them both. Was it O's silence, her meekness that endeared her to Anne-Marie? Scarcely had O's wounds healed than Anne-Marie remarked:

"How I regret not to be able to whip you! . . . When you come back . . . But let's say no more about it. In any event, I'm going to open you every day."

And, daily, when the girl who was in the music room had been untied, O would replace her until the bell rang for dinner. And Anne-Marie was right: it was true that during those two hours all she could think of was the fact that she was opened, and of the ring, hanging heavily from her (after one had been placed there) which, after they had inserted the second ring, weighed even more. She could think of nothing save her enslaved condition, and of the marks that went with it.

One evening Claire had come in with Colette from the garden, come over to O and examined both sides of the rings.

"When you went to Roissy," she said, "was it Anne-Marie who brought you there?"

"No," O said.

"It was Anne-Marie who brought me, two years ago. I'm going back there the day after tomorrow."

"But don't you belong to anyone?" O said.

"Claire belongs to me," said Anne-Marie, appearing from nowhere. "Your master's arriving tomorrow, O. Tonight you'll sleep with me."

The short summer night waxed slowly brighter until, toward four o'clock, daylight drowned the last stars. O, who was sleeping with her legs together, was awakened by Anne-Marie's hands probing between her thighs. But all Anne-Marie wanted was to awaken O, to have O caress her. Her eyes were shining in the half light, and her black hair, with the streaks of gray interspersed, was pushed up behind her on the pillow: only slightly curly, and cut quite short, it made her look like some mighty nobleman in exile, like some brave libertine. With her lips, O brushed the hard tips of her breasts, and her hand ran lightly over the valley of her belly. Anne-Marie was quick to yield—but not to O. The pleasure to which she opened her eyes wide, staring at the growing daylight, was an anonymous, impersonal pleasure of which O was merely the instrument. It made no difference whatever to Anne-Marie that O admired her face, smooth and glowing with renewed youth, her lovely panting lips, nor did she care whether O heard her moan when her lips and teeth seized the crest of flesh hidden in the furrow of her belly. She merely seized O by the hair to press her more closely to her, and only let her go in order to say to her:

"Again, do it again."

O had loved Jacqueline in the same way, had held her completely abandoned in her arms. She had possessed her; or at least so she thought. But the similarity of gestures meant nothing. O did not possess Anne-Marie. No one

159

possessed Anne-Marie. Anne-Marie demanded caresses without worrying about what the person providing them might feel, and she surrendered herself with an arrogant liberty. Yet she was all kindness and gentleness with O, kissed her on the mouth and kissed her breasts, and held her close against her for an hour before sending her back to her own room. She had removed her irons.

"These are your final hours here," she said, "you can sleep without the irons. The ones we'll put on you in a little while you'll never be able to take off."

She had run her hand softly, and at great length, over O's rear, then had taken her into the room where she, Anne-Marie, dressed, the only room in the house where there was a three-sided mirror. She had opened the mirror so that O could see herself.

"This is the last time you'll see yourself intact," she said. "Here, on this smooth, rounded area is where Sir Stephen's initials will be branded, on either side of the cleft in your behind. The day before you leave I'll bring you back here for another look at yourself. You won't recognize yourself. But Sir Stephen is right. Now go and get some sleep, O."

But O was too worried and upset to sleep, and when at ten the next morning Yvonne came to fetch her, O was trembling so that she had to help her bathe, arrange her hair, and put on her lipstick. She had heard the garden gate open; Sir Stephen was there.

"Come along now, O," Yvonne said, "he's waiting for you."

The sun was already high in the sky, not a breath of air was stirring in the leaves of the beech tree, which looked as though it were made out of copper. The dog, overcome by the heat, was lying at the foot of the tree, and since the sun had not yet disappeared behind the main mass of foliage, its rays shot through the end of the only branch which, at this hour, cast a shadow on the table: the marble top was resplendent with bright, warm spots of light.

Sir Stephen was standing, motionless, beside the table, Anne-Marie seated beside him.

"Here she is," said Anne-Marie, when Yvonne had brought O before them, "the rings can be put on whenever you like, she's been pierced."

Without replying, Sir Stephen took O in his arms, kissed her on the mouth and, lifting her completely off her feet, lay her down on the table and bent over her. Then he kissed her again, caressed her eyebrows and her hair and, straightening up, said to Anne-Marie:

"Right now, if it's all right with you."

Anne-Marie took the leather coffer which she had brought out with her and set down on a chair, and handed Sir Stephen the rings, which were unhooked, and on which were inscribed the names of O and Sir Stephen.

"Any time," Sir Stephen said.

Yvonne lifted O's knees, and O felt the cold metal as Anne-Marie slipped it into place. As she was slipping the second half of the ring into the first, she was careful to see that the side inlaid with gold was against her thigh, and the side which bore the inscription facing inward. But the spring was so tight that the prongs would not go in all the way. They had to send Yvonne to fetch the hammer. Then they made O sit up and lean over, with her legs spread, on the edge of the marble slab, which served as an anvil first for one then the other of the two links of the chain, while they hit the other end with a hammer to drive the prongs home. Sir Stephen looked on in silence. When it was over he thanked Anne-Marie and helped O to her feet. It was then she realized that these new irons were much heavier than the ones she had been wearing temporarily for the past few days. But these were permanent.

"And now your monogram, right?" Anne-Marie said to Sir Stephen.

Sir Stephen nodded assent, and held O by the waist, for she was stumbling and looked as though she might fall. She was not wearing her black corset, but it had so molded her into the desired shape that she looked as though she might break, so slim was her waistline now. And, as a result, her hips and breasts seemed fuller.

In the music room, into which Sir Stephen carried rather than led O, Colette and Claire were seated at the foot of the stage. When the others came in, they both got to their feet. On the stage was a big, round single-burner stove. Anne-Marie took the straps from the closet and had them tie O tightly around the waist and knees, her belly hard against one of the columns. They also bound her hands and feet. Consumed by fear and terror, O felt one of Anne-Marie's hands on her buttocks, indicating the exact spot for the irons, she heard the hiss of a flame and, in total silence, heard the window being closed. She could have turned her head and looked, but she did not have the strength to. One single, frightful stab of pain coursed through her, made her go rigid in her bonds and wrenched a scream from her lips, and she never knew who it was who had, with both branding irons at once, seared the flesh of her buttocks, nor whose voice had counted slowly up to five, nor whose hand had given the signal to withdraw the irons.

When they unfastened her, she collapsed into Anne-Marie's arms and had time, before everything turned black around her and she completely lost consciousness, to catch a glimpse, between two waves of darkness, of Sir Stephen's ghastly pale face.

162

Ten days before the end of July, Sir Stephen drove O back to Paris. The irons attached to the left lobe of her belly's cleft, proclaiming in bold letters that she was Sir Stephen's personal property, came about a third of the way down her thigh and, at every step, swung back and forth between her legs like the clapper of a bell, the inscribed disk being heavier and longer than the ring to which it was attached. The marks made by the branding iron, about three inches in height and half that in width, had been burned into the flesh as though by a gouging tool, and were almost half an inch deep: the lightest stroke of the finger revealed them. From these irons and these marks, O derived a feeling of inordinate pride. Had Jacqueline been there, instead of trying to conceal from her the fact that she bore them, as she had tried to hide the traces of the welts raised by the riding crop which Sir Stephen had wielded during those last days before her departure, she would have gone running in search of Jacqueline, to show them to her. But Jacqueline was not due back for another week. René wasn't there. During that week, O, at Sir Stephen's behest, had several summer dresses made, and a number of evening gowns of a very light material. He allowed her only two models, but let her order variations on both: one with a zipper all the way down the front (O already had several like it), the other a full skirt, easy to lift, always with a corselet above, which came up to below the breasts and was worn with a high-necked bolero. All one had to do was remove the bolero and the shoulders and breasts were bare, or simply to open it if one desired to see the breasts. Bathing suits, of course, were out of the question; the nether irons would hang below the suit. Sir Stephen had told her that this summer she would have to swim naked whenever she went swimming. Beach slacks were also out. However, Anne-

163

Marie, who was responsible for the two basic models of dresses, knowing where Sir Stephen's preference lay in using O, had proposed a type of slacks which would be supported in front by the blouse and, on both sides, have long zippers, thus allowing the back flap to be lowered without taking off the slacks. But Sir Stephen refused. It was true that he used O, when he did not have recourse to her mouth, almost invariably as he would have a boy. But O had had ample opportunity to notice that when she was near him, even when he did not particularly desire her, he loved to take hold of her womb, mechanically as it were, take hold of and tug at her fleece with his hand, to pry her open and burrow at length within. The pleasure O derived from holding Jacqueline in much the same way, moist and burning between her locked fingers, was ample evidence and a guarantee of Sir Stephen's pleasure. She understood why he did not want any extraneous obstacles set in the path of that pleasure.

Hatless, wearing practically no make-up, her hair completely free, O looked like a well-brought-up little girl, dressed as she was in her twilled stripe or polka dot, navy blue-and-white or gray-and-white pleated sun-skirts and the fitted bolero buttoned at the neck, or in her more conservative dresses of black nylon. Everywhere Sir Stephen escorted her she was taken for his daughter, or his niece, and this mistake was abetted by the fact that he, in addressing her, employed the *tu* form, whereas she employed the *vous*. Alone together in Paris, strolling through the streets to window shop, or walking along the quays, where the paving stones were dusty because the weather had been so dry, they evinced no surprise at seeing the passers-by smile at them, the way people smile at people who are happy.

Once in a while Sir Stephen would push her into the

recess of a porte-cochere, or beneath the archway of a building, which was always slightly dark, and from which there rose the musty odor of ancient cellars, and he would kiss her and tell her he loved her. O would hook her heels over the sill of the porte-cochere out of which the regular pedestrian door had been cut. They caught a glimpse of a courtyard in the rear, with lines of laundry drying in the windows. Leaning on one of the balconies, a blond girl would be staring fixedly at them. A cat would slip between their legs. Thus did they stroll through the Gobelins district, by Saint-Marcel, along the rue Mouffetard, to the area known as the Temple, and to the Bastille.

Once Sir Stephen suddenly steered O into a wretched brothel-like hotel, where the desk clerk first wanted them to fill out the forms, but then said not to bother if it was only for an hour. The wallpaper in the room was blue, with enormous golden peonies, the window looked out onto a pit whence rose the odor of garbage cans. However weak the light bulb at the head of the bed, you could still see streaks of face powder and forgotten hairpins on the mantelpiece. On the ceiling above the bed was a large mirror.

Once, but only once, Sir Stephen invited O to lunch with two of his compatriots who were passing through Paris. He came for her an hour before she was ready, and instead of having her driven to his place, he came to the quai de Bethune.

O had finished bathing, but she had not done her hair or put on her make-up, and was not dressed. To her surprise, she saw that Sir Stephen was carrying a golf bag, though she saw no clubs in it. But she soon got over her surprise: Sir Stephen told her to open the bag. Inside were several leather riding crops, two fairly thick ones of red leather, two that were long and thin of black leather, a scourge with long lashes of green leather, each of which was folded back at the end to form a loop, a dog's whip made of a thick, single lash whose handle was of braided leather and, last but not least, leather bracelets of the sort used at Roissy, plus some rope. O laid them out side by side on the unmade bed. No matter how accustomed she became to seeing them, no matter what resolutions she made about them, she could not keep from trembling. Sir Stephen took her in his arms.

"Which do you prefer, O?" he asked her.

But she could hardly speak, and already could feel the sweat running down her arms.

"Which do you prefer?" he repeated. "All right," he said, confronted by her silence, "first you're going to help me."

He asked her for some nails, and having found a way to arrange them in a decorative manner, whips and riding crops crossed, he showed O a panel of wainscoting between her mirror and the fireplace, opposite her bed, which would be ideal for them. He hammered some nails into the wood. There were rings on the ends of the handles of the whips and riding crops, by which they could be suspended from the nails, a system which allowed each whip to be easily taken down and returned to its place on the wall. Thus, together with the bracelets and the rope, O would have, opposite her bed, the complete array of her instruments of torture. It was a handsome panoply, as harmonious as the wheel and spikes in the paintings of Saint Catherine the Martyr, as the nails and hammer, the crown of thorns, the spear and scourges portrayed in the paintings of the Crucifixion. When Jacqueline came back . . . but all this involved Jacqueline, involved her deeply. She would have to reply to Sir Stephen's question: O could not, he chose the dog whip himself.

In a tiny private dining room of the La Pérouse restaurant, along the quays of the Left Bank, a room on the third floor whose dark walls were brightened by Watteau-like figures in pastel colors who resembled actors of the puppet theater, O was ensconced alone on the sofa, with one of Sir Stephen's friends in an armchair to her right, another to her left, and Sir Stephen across from her. She remembered already having seen one of the men at Roissy, but she could not recall having been taken by him. The other was a tall, red-haired boy with gray eyes, who could not have been more than twenty-five. In two words, Sir Stephen told them why he had invited O, and what she was. Listening to him, O was once again astonished at the coarseness of his language. But then, how did she expect to be referred to, if not as a whore, a girl who, in the presence of three men (not to mention the restaurant waiters who kept trooping in and out, since luncheon was still being served) would open her bodice to bare her breasts, the tips of which had been reddened with lipstick, as they could see, as they could also see from the purple furrows across her milk-white skin that she had been flogged?

The meal went on for a long time, and the two Englishmen drank a great deal. Over coffee, when the liqueurs had been served, Sir Stephen pushed the table back against the opposite wall and, after having lifted her skirt to show his friends how O was branded and in irons, left her to them.

The man she had met at Roissy wasted no time with her: without leaving his armchair, without even touching her with his fingertips, he ordered her to kneel down in front of him, take him and caress his sex until he discharged in her mouth. After which, he made her straighten out his clothing, and then he left.

But the red-haired lad, who had been completely overwhelmed by O's submissiveness and meek surrender, by her irons and the welts which he had glimpsed on her body, took her by the hand instead of throwing himself upon her as she had expected, and descended the stairs, paying not the slightest heed to the sly smiles of the waiters and, after hailing a taxi, took her back to his hotel room. He did not let her go till nightfall, after having frantically plowed her fore and aft, both of which he bruised and belabored unmercifully, he being of an uncommon size and rigidity and, what is more, being totally intoxicated by the sudden freedom granted him to penetrate a woman doubly and be embraced by her in the way he had seen her ordered to a short while before (something he had never before dared ask of anyone).

The following day, when O arrived at Sir Stephen's at two o'clock in answer to his summons, she found him looking older and his face careworn.

"Eric has fallen head over heels in love with you, O," he told her. "This morning he called on me and begged me to grant you your freedom. He told me he wants to marry you. He wants to save you. You see how I treat you if you're mine, O, and if you are mine you have no right to refuse my commands; but you also know that you are always free to choose *not* to be mine. I told him so. He's coming back here at three."

O burst out laughing. "Isn't it a little late?" she said. "You're both quite mad. If Eric had not come by this morning, what would you have done with me this afternoon? We would have gone for a walk, nothing more? Then let's go for a walk. Or perhaps you would not have summoned me this afternoon? In that case I'll leave. . . ."

"No," Sir Stephen broke in, "I would have called you, but not to go for a walk. I wanted . . ."

"Go on, say it."

"Come, it will be simpler to show you."

He got up and opened a door in the wall opposite the fireplace, a door identical to the one into his office.

O had always thought that the door led into a closet which was no longer used. She saw a tiny bedroom, newly painted, and hung with dark red silk. Half of the room was occupied by a rounded stage flanked by two columns, identical to the stage in the music room at Samois.

"The walls and ceiling are lined with cork, are they not?" O said. "And the door is padded, and you've had a double window installed?"

Sir Stephen nodded.

"But since when has all this been done?" O said.

"Since you've been back."

"Then why? . . ."

"Why did I wait until today? Because I first wanted to hand you over to other men. Now I shall punish you for it. I've never punished you, O."

"But I belong to you," O said. "Punish me. When Eric comes . . ."

An hour later, when he was shown a grotesquely bound and spread-eagled O strapped to the two columns, the boy blanched, mumbled something, and disappeared. O thought she would never see him again. She ran into him again at Roissy, at the end of September, and he had her consigned to him for three days in a row, during which he savagely abused and mistreated her.

IV

The Owl

What O failed completely to understand now was why she had ever been hesitant to speak to Jacqueline about what René rightly called her true condition. Anne-Marie had warned her that she would be changed when she left Samois, but O had never imagined the change would be so great. With Jacqueline back, more lovely and radiant than ever, it seemed natural to her to be no more reticent about revealing herself when she bathed or dressed than she was when she was alone. And yet Jacqueline was so disinterested in others, in anything that did not pertain directly to herself, that it was not until the second day after Jacqueline arrived back and by chance came into the bathroom just as O was stepping out of the tub, that O jingled her irons against the porcelain to draw her attention to the odd noise. Jacqueline turned her head, and saw both the disk hanging between her legs and the black stripes crisscrossing her thighs and breasts.

"What in the world's the matter?" she said.

"It's Sir Stephen," O replied. And she added, as though it were something to be taken completely for granted: "René gave me to him, and he's had me pierced with his

173

rings. Look." And as she dried herself with the bath towel she came over to Jacqueline, who was so staggered she had slumped onto the lacquered bathroom stool, close enough so that Jacqueline could take the disk in her hand and read the inscription; then, slipping down her bathrobe she turned around and pointed to the initials S and H engraved in her buttocks and said:

"He also had me branded with his monogram. As for the rest, that's where I was flogged with a riding crop. He generally whips me himself, but he also has a Negro maid whip me."

Dumbfounded, Jacqueline gazed at O. O burst out laughing and made as though to kiss her. Terror-stricken, Jacqueline pushed her away and fled into her own room. O leisurely finished drying herself, put on her perfume, and combed her hair. She put on her corset, her stockings, her mules, and when she opened the bathroom door she encountered Jacqueline's gaze in the mirror, before which she was combing her hair, without having the vaguest notion what she was doing.

"Lace up my corset, will you?" she said. "You really do look astonished. René's in love with you, didn't he say anything to you about it?"

"I don't understand," Jacqueline said. And she lost no time revealing what surprised her the most. "You look as though you were proud of it, I don't understand."

"You will, after René takes you to Roissy. By the way, have you already slept with him?"

Jacqueline's face turned a bright crimson, and she was shaking her head in denial with such little conviction that once again O burst out laughing.

"You're lying, darling, don't be an ass. You have every right in the world to sleep with him. And I might add that

174

that's no reason to reject me. Come, let me caress you and I'll tell you all about Roissy."

Had Jacqueline been afraid that O's jealousy would explode in her face and then yield to her out of relief when it did not, or was it curiosity, did she want to hear the promised explanations, or was it merely because she loved the patience, the slowness, the passion of O's caresses? In any event, yield she did.

"Tell me about it," she later said to O.

"All right," O said. "But first kiss the tips of my breasts. It's time you got used to it, if you're ever to be of any use to René."

Jacqueline did as she was bade, so well in fact that she wrested a moan from O.

"Tell me about it," she said.

O's tale, however faithful and clear it may have been, and notwithstanding the material proof she herself constituted, seemed completely mad to Jacqueline.

"You mean you're going back in September?" she said.

"After we've come back from the Midi," O said. "I'll take you, or René will."

"To see what it's like, I wouldn't mind that," Jacqueline went on, "but only to see what it's like."

"I'm sure that can be arranged," said O, though she was convinced of the contrary. But, she kept telling herself, if she could only persuade Jacqueline to enter the gates at Roissy, Sir Stephen would be grateful to her—and once she was in, there would be enough valets, chains, and whips to teach Jacqueline to obey.

She already knew that the summer house that Sir Stephen had rented near Cannes on the Riviera, where she was scheduled to spend the month of August with René, Jacqueline, and him (and with Jacqueline's younger sister, whom Jacqueline had asked if she could bring along, not because she cared especially to have her but because her mother had been hounding her to obtain O's permission), she knew that her room, to which she was certain she could entice Jacqueline, who would be unable to refuse when René was away, was separated from Sir Stephen's bedroom by a wall that looked as though it was full but actually was not; the wall was decorated with a trompe l'oeil latticework which enabled Sir Stephen to raise a blind on his side and thus to see and hear as well as if he had been standing beside the bed. Jacqueline would be surrendered to Sir Stephen's gaze while O was caressing her, and by the time she found out it would be too late. O was pleased to think that she would deliver Jacqueline by an act of betrayal, because she had felt insulted at seeing Jacqueline's contempt for her condition as a flogged and branded slave, a condition of which O herself was proud.

O had never been to the south of France before. The clear blue sky, the almost mirror-like sea, the motionless pines beneath the burning sun: everything seemed mineral and hostile to her. "No real trees," she remarked sadly to herself as she gazed at the fragrant thickets full of shrubs and bushes, where all the stones, and even the lichens, were warm to the touch. "The sea doesn't smell like the sea," she thought. She blamed the sea for washing up nothing more than an occasional piece of wretched seaweed which looked like dung, she blamed it for being too blue and for always lapping at the same bit of shore. But in the garden of Sir Stephen's villa, which was an old farmhouse that had been restored, they were far from the sea. To left and right, high walls protected them from the neighbors; the servants' wing faced the entrance courtyard, while the side of the house overlooking the garden faced the east; O's bedroom was on this side, and opened directly onto a second-story terrace. The tops of the tall black cypress trees were level with the overlapping hollow tiles which served as a parapet for the terrace, which was protected from the noon sun by a reed latticework. The floor of the terrace was of red tile, the same as the tiles in her bedroom. Aside from the wall which separated O's bedroom from Sir Stephen's—and this was the wall of a large alcove bounded by an archway and separated from the rest of the room by a kind of railing similar to the railings of stairways, with banisters of hand-carved wood —all the other walls were whitewashed. The thick white rug on the tile floor was made of cotton, the curtains were of yellow-and-white linen. There were two armchairs upholstered in the same material, and some triple-layered Oriental cushions. The only furniture was a heavy and very handsome Regency bureau made of walnut, and a very long, narrow peasant table in light-colored wood which was waxed till it shone like a mirror. O hung her clothes in a closet. For a dressing table, she used the top of the bureau.

Jacqueline's little sister Natalie had been given a room near O's, and in the morning when she knew that O was taking a sunbath on the terrace, she came out and lay down beside her. She had snow-white skin, was a shade plump, but her features were none the less delicate and, like her sister, she had slanting eyes, but hers were black and shining, which made her look Chinese. Her black hair was cut in straight bangs across her forehead, just above her eyebrows, and in the back was also cut straight, at the nape of the neck. She had firm, tremulous little breasts, and her adolescent hips were only beginning to fill out. She too had chanced upon O, and taken her quite by surprise, one day when she had dashed out onto the ter-

177

race expecting to find her sister but found O instead, lying there alone on her stomach on the Oriental pillows. But what had shocked Jacqueline filled Natalie with envy and desire. She asked her sister about it. Jacqueline's replies, which were intended to shock and revolt young Natalie by repeating to her what O had related, in no wise altered Natalie's feelings. If anything, it accomplished the contrary. She had fallen in love with O. For more than a week she managed to keep it to herself, then late one Sunday afternoon she managed to be alone with O.

The weather had been cooler than normal. René, who had spent part of the morning swimming, was asleep on the sofa of a cool room on the ground floor. Nettled at seeing that he should prefer to take a nap, Jacqueline had gone upstairs and joined O in her alcove. The sea and sun had already made her more golden than before: her hair, her eyebrows, her eyelashes, her nether fleece, her armpits, all seemed to be powdered with silver, and since she was not wearing any make-up, her mouth was the same color pink as the pink flesh between her thighs.

To make sure that Sir Stephen could see Jacqueline in detail—and O thought to herself that if she were Jacqueline she would have guessed, or noticed, his invisible presence—O took pains to pull back her legs and keep them spread in the light of the bedside lamp which she had turned on. The shutters were closed, the room almost dark, despite the thin rays of light that spilled in where the wood was not snug. For more than an hour Jacqueline moaned to O's caresses, and finally, her breasts aroused, her arms thrown back behind her head while her hands circled the wooden bars of the headboard of O's Italian-style bed, she began to cry out when O, parting the lobes hemmed with pale hair, slowly began to bite the crest of flesh at the point between her thighs where the dainty, supple lips joined. O felt her rigid and burning beneath her tongue, and wrested cry after cry from her lips, with no respite, until she suddenly relaxed, the springs broken, and she lay there moist with pleasure. Then O sent her back to her room, where she fell asleep.

Jacqueline was awake and ready, though, when René came for her at five o'clock to go sailing, with Natalie, in a small sailboat, as they had grown accustomed to doing. A slight wind usually came up at the end of the afternoon.

"Where's Natalie?" René said.

Natalie was not in her room, nor was she anywhere in the house. They went out to the garden and called her. René went as far as the thicket of scrub oak at the end of the garden; no one answered.

"Maybe she's already down at the inlet," René said, "or in the boat."

They left without calling her any more.

It was at that point that O, who was lying on the Oriental pillows on her terrace, glanced through the tile banisters and saw Natalie running toward the house. She got up, put on her dressing gown—it was still so warm, even this late in the afternoon, that she was naked—and was tying her belt when Natalie erupted into the room like one of the Furies and threw herself at O.

"She's gone," she shouted, "she's finally gone. I heard her, O, I heard you both, I was listening behind the door. You kiss her, you caress her. Why don't you caress me, why don't you kiss me? Is it because I'm dark, because I'm not pretty? She doesn't love you, O, but I do, I love you!" And she broke down and began to sob.

"All right, fine," O said to herself.

She eased the child into an armchair, took a large handkerchief from her bureau (it was one of Sir Stephen's), and when Natalie's sobs had subsided a little, wiped her

179

tears away. Natalie begged her forgiveness, kissing O's hands.

"Even if you don't want to kiss me, O, keep me with you. Keep me with you always. If you had a dog, you'd keep him and take care of him. And even if you don't want to kiss me but would enjoy beating me, you can beat me. But don't send me away."

"Keep still, Natalie, you don't know what you're saying," O murmured, almost in a whisper.

The child, slipping down and hugging O's knees, also replied in a near-whisper:

"Oh, yes I do. I saw you the other morning on the terrace. I saw the initials, I saw the long black-and-blue marks. And Jacqueline has told me . . ."

"Told you what?"

"Where you've been, O, and what they did to you there."

"Did she talk to you about Roissy?"

"She also told me that you had been, that you are . . ."

"That I was what?"

"That you wear iron rings."

"That's right," O said, "and what else?"

"That Sir Stephen whips you every day."

"That's correct," O repeated, "and he'll be here any second. So run along, Natalie."

Natalie, without shifting position, raised her head to O, and O's eyes encountered her adoring gaze.

"Teach me, O, please teach me," she started in again, "I want to be like you. I'll do anything you tell me. Promise me you'll take me with you when you go back to that place Jacqueline told me about."

"You're too young," O said.

"No, I'm not too young, I'm fifteen going on sixteen,"

she cried out angrily. "I'm not too young. Ask Sir Stephen," she said, for he had just entered the room.

Natalie was granted permission to remain with O, and extracted the promise that she would be taken to Roissy. But Sir Stephen forbade O to teach her the least caress, not even a kiss on the lips, and also gave strict instructions that O was not to allow Natalie to kiss her. He had every intention of having her reach Roissy completely untouched by hands or lips. By way of compensation, what he did demand, since Natalie was loath to leave O, was that she not leave her for a single moment, that she witness O caressing both Jacqueline and himself, that she be present when O yielded to him and when he whipped her, or when she was flogged by old Norah. The kisses with which O smothered her sister, O's mouth glued to hers, made Natalie quiver with jealousy and hate. But, cowering on the carpet in the alcove, at the foot of O's bed, like little Dinarzade at the foot of Scheherazade's bed, she watched each time that O, tied to the wooden balustrade, writhed and squirmed beneath the riding crop, saw O on her knees humbly receiving Sir Stephen's massive, upright sex in her mouth, saw her, prostrate, spread her own buttocks with both hands to offer him the after passage—she witnessed all these things with no other feelings but those of admiration, envy, and impatience.

It was about this same time that a change took place in Jacqueline: perhaps O had counted too heavily both on Jacqueline's indifference and her sensuality, perhaps Jacqueline herself naively felt that surrendering herself to O was dangerous for her relations with René; but whatever the reason, she suddenly ceased coming to O. At the same time, she seemed to be keeping herself aloof from René, with whom, however, she was spending almost every day and every night. She had never acted as though she were in love with him. She studied him coldly, and when she smiled at him, her eyes remained cold. Even assuming that she was as completely abandoned with him as she was with O, which was quite likely, O could not help thinking that this surrender was superficial. Whereas René was head over heels in love with her, paralyzed by a love such as he had never known before, a worrisome, uncertain love, one he was far from sure was requited, a love that acts not, for fear of offending. He lived, he slept in the same house as Sir Stephen, the same house as O, he lunched, he dined, he went on walks with Sir Stephen, with O, he conversed with them both: he didn't see them, he didn't hear what they said. He saw, he heard, he talked through them, beyond them, and, as in a dream when one tries to catch a departing train or clings desperately to the parapet of a collapsing bridge, he was forever trying to understand the *raison d'être*, the truth which must have been lurking somewhere inside Jacqueline, under that golden skin, like the mechanism inside a crying doll.

"Well," thought O, "the day I was so afraid would arrive is here, the day when I'd merely be a shadow in René's past. And I'm not even sad; the only thing I feel for him is pity, and even knowing he doesn't desire me any longer, I can see him every day without any trace of bitterness, without the least regret, without even feeling hurt. And yet only a few weeks ago I dashed all the way across town to his office, to beg him to tell me he still loved me. Was that all my love was, all it meant? So light, so easily gone and forgotten? Is solace that simple? And solace is not even the right word: I'm happy. Do you mean to say it was enough for him to have given me to Sir Stephen for me to be detached from him, for me to find a new love so easily in the arms of another?"

But then, what was René compared to Sir Stephen?

Ropes of straw, anchors of cork, paper chains: these were the real symbols of the bonds with which he had held her, and which he had been so quick to sever. But what a delight and comfort, this iron ring which pierces the flesh and weighs one down forever, this mark eternal, how peaceful and reassuring the hand of a master who lays you on a bed of rock, the love of a master who knows how to take what he loves ruthlessly, without pity. And O said to herself that, in the final analysis, with René she had been an apprentice to love, she had loved him only to learn how to give herself, enslaved and surfeited, to Sir Stephen. But to see René, who had been so free with her —and she had loved his free ways—walking as though he were hobbled, like someone whose legs were ensnarled in the water and reeds of a pond whose surface seems calm but which, deeper down, swirls with subterranean currents, to see him thus, filled O with hate for Jacqueline. Did René dimly perceive her feelings? Did O carelessly reveal how she felt? In any case, O committed an error.

One afternoon she and Jacqueline had gone to Cannes together to the hairdresser, alone, then to the Reserve Café for an ice cream on the terrace. Jacqueline was superb in her tight-fitting black slacks and sheer black sweater, eclipsing even the brilliance of the children around her she was so bronzed and sleek, so hard and bright in the burning sun, so insolent and inaccessible. She told O she had made an appointment there with the director whose picture she had been playing in in Paris, to arrange for taking some exteriors, probably in the mountains above Saint-Paul-de-Vence. And there he was, forthright and determined. He didn't need to open his mouth, it was obvious he was in love with Jacqueline. All one had to do was see the way he looked at her. What was so surprising about that? Nothing; but what was surprising was Jacqueline. Half reclining in one of those adjustable beach chairs, Jacqueline listened to him as he talked of dates to be set, appointments to be made, of the problems of raising enough money to finish the half-completed picture. He used the *tu* form in addressing Jacqueline, who replied with a mere nod or shake of her head, keeping her eyes half-closed. O was seated across from Jacqueline, with him between them. It took no great act of perception to notice that Jacqueline, whose eyes were still lowered, was watching, from beneath the protection of those motionless eyelids, the young man's desire, the way she always did when she thought no one was looking. But strangest of all was how upset she seemed, her hands quiet at her side, her face serious and expressionless, without the trace of a smile, something she had never displayed in René's presence. A fleeting, almost imperceptible smile on her lips as O leaned forward to set her glass of ice water on the table and their eyes met, was all O needed to realize that Jacqueline was aware that O knew the game was up. It didn't bother her, though; it was rather O who blushed.

"Are you too warm?" Jacqueline said. "We'll be leaving in five minutes. Red is becoming to you, by the way."

Then she smiled again, turning her gaze to her interlocutor, a smile so utterly tender that it seemed impossible he would not hasten to embrace her. But he did not. He was too young to know that motionlessness and silence can be the lair of immodesty. He allowed Jacqueline to get up, shook hands with her, and said good-by. She would phone him. He also said good-by to the shadow that O represented for him, and stood on the sidewalk watching the black Buick disappear down the avenue between the sun-drenched houses and the dark, almost purple sea. The palm trees looked as though they had been cut out of metal, the strollers like poorly fashioned wax models, animated by some absurd mechanism.

"You really like him all that much?" O said to Jacqueline as the car left the city and moved along the upper coast road.

"Is that any business of yours?" Jacqueline responded.

"It's René's business," she retorted.

"What is René's business, and Sir Stephen's, and, if I understand it correctly, a number of other people's, is the fact you're badly seated. You're going to wrinkle your dress."

O failed to move.

"And I also thought," Jacqueline added, "that you weren't supposed to cross your legs."

But O was no longer listening. What did she care about Jacqueline's threats? If Jacqueline threatened to inform on her for that peccadillo, what did she think would keep her from denouncing Jacqueline in turn to René? Not that O lacked the desire to. But René would not be able to bear the news that Jacqueline was lying to him, or that she had plans of her own which did not include him. How could she make Jacqueline believe that if she were to keep still, it would be to avoid seeing René lose face, turning pale over someone other than herself, and perhaps revealing himself to be too weak to punish her? How could she convince her that her silence, even more, would be the result of her fear at seeing René's wrath turned against her, the bearer of ill tidings, the informer? How could she tell Jacqueline that she would not say a word, without giving the impression she was making a mutual non-betrayal pact with her? For Jacqueline had the idea that O was terrified, terrified to death at what would happen to her if she, Jacqueline, talked.

From that point on, until they got out of the car in the

courtyard of the old farm, they did not exchange another word. Without glancing at O, Jacqueline picked a white geranium growing beside the house. O was following closely enough behind to catch a whiff of the strong, delicate odor of the leaf crumpled between her hands. Did she believe she would thus be able to mask the odor of her own sweat, which was making darkening circles beneath the arms of her sweater and causing the black material to cling to her armpits.

In the big whitewashed room with the red-tile floor, René was alone.

"You're late," he said when they came in. "Sir Stephen's waiting for you in the next room," he added, nodding to O. "He needs you for something. He's not in a very good mood."

Jacqueline burst out laughing, and O looked at her and turned red.

"You could have saved it for another time," said René, who misinterpreted both Jacqueline's laugh and O's concern.

"That's not the reason," Jacqueline said, "but I might say, René, your obedient beauty isn't so obedient when you're not around. Look at her dress, you see how wrinkled it is?"

O was standing in the middle of the room, facing René. He told her to turn around; she was rooted to the spot.

"She also crosses her legs," Jacqueline added, "but that you won't be able to see, of course. As you won't be able to see the way she accosts the boys."

"That's not true," O shouted, "you're the one!" and she leaped at Jacqueline.

René grabbed her just as she was about to hit Jacqueline, and she went on struggling in his arms merely for the sake of feeling weaker than he, of being at his mercy, when, lifting her head, she saw Sir Stephen standing in the doorway looking at her.

Jacqueline had thrown herself down on the sofa, her tiny face hardened with anger and fear, and O could feel that René, though he had his hands full trying to subdue her, had eyes only for Jacqueline. She ceased resisting and, crestfallen at the idea of having been found wanting in the presence of Sir Stephen, she repeated, this time almost in a whisper:

"It's not true, I swear it's not true."

Without uttering a word, without so much as a glance at Jacqueline, Sir Stephen made a sign to René to let O go, and to O to go into the other room. But on the other side of the door O, who was immediately wedged against the wall, her belly and breasts seized, her lips forced apart by Sir Stephen's insistent tongue, moaned with happiness and deliverance. The points of her breasts stiffened beneath his hand's caress, and with his other hand Sir Stephen probed her loins so roughly she thought she would faint. Would she ever dare tell him that no pleasure, no joy, no figment of her imagination could ever compete with the happiness she felt at the way he used her with such utter freedom, at the notion that he could do anything with her, that there was no limit, no restriction in the manner with which, on her body, he might search for pleasure. Her absolute certainty that when he touched her, whether it was to fondle or flog her, when he ordered her to do something it was solely because he wanted to, her certainty that all he cared about was his own desire, so overwhelmed and gratified O that each time she saw a new proof of it, and often even when it merely occurred to her in thought, a cape of fire, a burning breastplate extending from the shoulders to the knees, descended upon her. As she was there, pinned against the wall, her eyes closed,

187

her lips murmuring "I love you" when she could find the breath to say them, Sir Stephen's hands, though they were as cool as the waters of a bubbling spring on the fire coursing through her from head to toe, made her burn even hotter. Gently he released her, dropping her skirt down over her moist thighs, closing her bolero over her quivering breasts.

"Come, O," he said, "I need you."

Then, opening her eyes, O noticed that they were not alone. The big, bare, whitewashed room, identical in all respects to the living room, also opened, through a French door, onto the garden. Seated in a wicker chair on the terrace, which lay between the house and garden, an enormous man, a giant of a creature with a cigarette between his lips, his head shaved and his vast belly swelling beneath his open shirt and cloth trousers, was gazing at O. He rose and moved toward Sir Stephen, who was shoving O ahead of him. It was then that O noticed, dangling at the end of his watch chain, the Roissy insignia that the man was sporting. Still, Sir Stephen politely introduced him to O, simply as "Commander," with no name attached, and much to O's surprise she saw that he was kissing her hand, the first time it had happened since she had been involved with Roissy members (with the exception of Sir Stephen).

All three of them came back into the room, leaving the door open. Sir Stephen walked over to one end of the fireplace and rang. On the Chinese table beside the sofa, O saw a bottle of whisky, some soda water, and glasses. So he was not ringing for something to drink. At the same time she noticed a large cardboard box on the floor beside the fireplace. The man from Roissy had sat down on a wicker chair, Sir Stephen was half-seated on the edge of the round table, with one leg dangling. O, who had been motioned over to the sofa, had meekly raised her skirt and could feel the prickly cotton of the roughly woven Provençal upholstery.

It was Norah who came in. Sir Stephen ordered her to undress O and remove her clothing from the room. O allowed her to take off her bolero, her dress, her whalebone belt which constricted her waist, and her sandals. As soon as she had stripped O completely, Norah left, and O, automatically reverting to the rules of Roissy, and certain that all Sir Stephen wanted from her was perfect submissiveness, remained standing in the middle of the room, her eyes lowered, so that she sensed rather than saw Natalie slip in through the open window, dressed in black like her sister, barefoot and silent. Sir Stephen had doubtless explained who she was and why she was there; to his visitor he merely mentioned her name, to which the visitor did not respond, and asked her to make them a drink. As soon as she had handed them some whisky, soda water, and ice cubes (and, in the silence, the clink of the ice cubes against the sides of the glasses made a harrowing racket), the Commander got up from his wicker chair, in which he had been sitting while O was being undressed and, with his glass in his hand, walked over to O. O thought that, with his free hand, he was going to take her breast or seize her belly. But he did not touch her, confining himself to scrutinizing her closely, from her parted lips to her parted knees. He circled her, studying her breasts, her thighs, her hindquarters, inspecting her in detail but offering no comment, and this careful scrutiny and the presence of this gigantic body so close to her so overwhelmed O that she wasn't sure whether she wanted to run away or, on the contrary, have him throw her down and crush her. So upset was she that she lost control and raised her eyes toward Sir Stephen, searching for help. He understood, smiled, came over to her, and, taking both her hands, pulled them behind her back, and held them in one of his. She leaned back against him, her eyes closed, and it was in a dream, or at least in the dusk of a near-sleep born of exhaustion, the way she had heard as a child, still half under the influence of ether, the nurses talking about her, thinking she was still asleep, of her hair, her pallor, her flat belly where only the faint early signs of pubescence were showing, it was in a dream that she heard the stranger complimenting Sir Stephen on her, paying special due to the pleasant contrast between her ample bosom and the narrow waist, the irons which he found longer, thicker, and more visible than usual. At the same time, she learned that Sir Stephen had in all probability consented to lend her to him the following week, since he was thanking Sir Stephen for something. At which point Sir Stephen, taking her by the nape of the neck, gently told her to wake up and, with Natalie, to go upstairs and wait in her room.

Had she good reason to be so upset, and to be so annoyed at Natalie who, elated at the prospect of seeing O opened by someone other than Sir Stephen, was doing a kind of wild Indian dance around her and shouting:

"Do you think he'll go into your mouth too, O? You should have seen the way he was looking at your mouth! Oh, how lucky you are to be desired like that! I'm sure that he'll whip you: he came back three times to those marks where you can see you've been whipped. At least you won't be thinking about Jacqueline then!"

"I'm not always thinking about Jacqueline, you silly fool," O replied.

"No! I'm not silly and I'm not a fool. I know very well you miss her," the child said.

It was true, but not completely. What O missed was not, properly speaking, Jacqueline, but the use of a girl's body, with no restrictions attached. If Natalie had not been declared off-limits to her, she would have taken Natalie, and the only reason she had not violated the restriction was her certainty that Natalie would be given to her at Roissy in a few weeks' time, and that, some time previously, Natalie would be handed over in her presence, by her, and thanks to her. She was burning to demolish the wall of air, of space, of—to use the only correct term—void between Natalie and her, and yet at the same time she was enjoying the wait imposed upon her. She said so to Natalie, who only shook her head and refused to believe her.

"If Jacqueline were here, and were willing," she said, "you'd caress her."

"Of course I would," O said with a laugh.

"There, you see," the child broke in.

How could she make her understand—and was it even worth the effort?—that it wasn't so much that she was in love with Jacqueline, nor for that matter with Natalie or any other girl in particular, but that she was only in love with girls as such, girls in general—the way one can be in love with one's own image—but in her case she always thought the other girls were more lovely and desirable than she found herself to be. The pleasure she derived from seeing a girl pant beneath her caresses, seeing her eyes close and the tips of her breasts stiffen beneath her lips and teeth, the pleasure she got from exploring her fore and aft with her hand—and from feeling her tighten around her fingers, then sigh and moan—was more than she could bear; and if this pleasure was so intense, it was only because it made her constantly aware of the pleasure which she in turn gave when she tightened around whoever was holding her, whenever she sighed or moaned, with this difference, that she could not conceive of being

191

given thus to a girl, the way this girl was given to her, but only to a man. Moreover, it seemed to her that the girls she caressed belonged by right to the man to whom she belonged, and that she was only present by proxy. Had Sir Stephen come into her room during one of those previous afternoons when Jacqueline had been wont to nap with her, and found O caressing her, she would have spread her charge's thighs and held them apart with both hands, without the slightest remorse, and in fact with the greatest of pleasure, if it had pleased Sir Stephen to possess her, rather than peering at her through the trellised wall as he had done. She was apt at hunting, a naturally trained bird of prey who would beat the game and always bring it back to the hunter. And speaking of the devil . . .

It was at this point, just as she was thinking again with beating heart of Jacqueline's lips, so pink and dainty beneath her downy fur, of the even more delicate and pinker ring between her buttocks, which she had only dared force on three occasions, that she heard Sir Stephen moving about in his room. She knew that he could see her, although she could not see him, and once again she felt that she was fortunate indeed to be constantly exposed this way, constantly imprisoned by these all-encompassing eyes. Young Natalie was seated on the white rug in the middle of the room, like a fly in a bowl of milk; while O, standing in front of the massive bureau which also served as her dressing table, and able to see herself from head to waist in a slightly greenish antique mirror which was streaked like the wrinkles in a pond, looked for all the world like one of those late nineteenth-century prints in which the women are wandering naked through their chambers in a subdued light, even though it is mid-summer.

When Sir Stephen pushed open the door, she turned

around so abruptly that one of the irons between her legs struck one of the bronze knobs of the bureau upon which she was leaning, and jingled.

"Natalie," Sir Stephen said, "run downstairs and get the white cardboard box in the front living room."

When Natalie came back, she set the box down on the bed, opened it, and one by one removed the objects inside, unwrapping the paper in which they were packed, and handing them to Sir Stephen. They were masks, a combination headpiece and mask; it was obvious they had been made to cover the entire head, with the exception of the mouth and chin—and of course the slits for eyes. Sparrow-hawk, falcon, owl, fox, lion, bull: nothing but animal masks, but scaled to the size of the human head, made of real fur and feathers, the eye crowned with lashes when the actual animal had lashes (as the lion), and with the pelts or feathers descending to the shoulders of the person wearing them. To make the mask fit snugly along the upper lips (there was an orifice for each nostril) and along both cheeks, all one had to do was adjust a fairly loose strap concealed inside this cope-like affair which hung down the back. A frame made of molded, hardened cardboard located between the outside facing and the inner lining of skin, kept the shape of the mask rigid. In front of the full-length mirror, O tried on each of the masks. The most striking, and the one she thought transformed her most and was also most natural, was one of the owl masks (there were two), no doubt because it was composed of tan and tawny feathers whose color blended beautifully with her tan; the cope of feathers almost completely concealed her shoulders, descending half way down her back and, in front, to the nascent curve of her breasts. Sir Stephen had her rub the lipstick from her lips, then said to her as she took off the mask:

"All right, you'll be an owl for the Commander. But O, and I hope you forgive me, you'll be taken on a leash. Natalie, go look in the top drawer of my desk, you'll find a chain and a pair of pliers."

Natalie came back with the chain and pliers, which Sir Stephen used to force open the last link, fastened it to the second ring that O was wearing in her loins, then forced it closed again. The chain, similar to those used for dogs—in fact that was what it was—was between four and five feet long, with a leather strap on one end. After O had again donned the mask, Sir Stephen told Natalie to take the end of the chain and walk around the room, ahead of O. Three times Natalie paraded around the room, trailing O behind her by the rings, O being naked and masked.

"Well, I must say," Sir Stephen remarked, "the Commander was right, all the hair will have to be removed. But that can wait till tomorrow. Meanwhile, keep your chain on."

That evening, and for the first time in the company of Jacqueline and Natalie, of René and Sir Stephen, O dined naked, her chain pulled up between her legs and across her buttocks and wrapped around her waist. Norah was alone serving, and O avoided her gaze. Two hours before, Sir Stephen had summoned her.

What shocked and upset the girl at the beauty parlor the following day, more than the irons and the black and blue marks on her lower back, were the brand new lacerations. O had gone there to have the offending hair removed, and it did no good to explain to her that this wax-type depilatory, a method in which the wax is applied and allowed to harden, then suddenly removed, taking the hair with it—was no more painful than being struck with the riding crop. No matter how many times she repeated it, or made an attempt to explain, if not what her fate was, at least that she was happy, there was no way of reassuring her or allaying her feeling of disgust and terror. The only visible result of O's efforts to soothe her was that, instead of being looked upon with pity, as she had been at first, she was beheld with horror. It made no difference how kind and profuse were her thanks when she left the little alcove where she had been spread-eagled as though for love, nor did it matter how generous a tip she gave as she left, when it was all over, she had the feeling that she was being evicted rather than leaving of her own free will. What did she care? It was obvious to her that there was something shocking about the contrast between the fur on her belly and the feathers on her mask, as it was obvious that this air of an Egyptian statue which this mask lent her, and which her broad shoulders, narrow waist, and long legs only served to emphasize, to demand that her flesh be perfectly smooth. Only the effigies of primitive goddesses portrayed so proudly and openly the cleft of the belly between whose outer lips appeared the more delicate line of the lower lips. And had any ever been seen sporting rings in their nether lips? O recalled the plump, red-haired girl at Anne-Marie's who had said that all her master ever used the belly ring for was to attach her to the foot of the bed, and she had also said that the reason he wanted her shaved was because only in that way was she completely naked. O was worried about displeasing Sir Stephen, who so enjoyed pulling her over to him by the fleece, but she was mistaken: Sir Stephen found her more moving that way, and after she had donned her mask, having removed all trace of lipstick above and below, the upper and nether lips then being so uncommonly pale, that he caressed her almost timidly, the way one does with an animal one wants to tame.

He had told her nothing about the place to which he

195

was taking her, nor indicated the time they would have to leave, nor had he said who the Commander's guests would be. But he came and spent the rest of the afternoon sleeping beside her, and in the evening had dinner brought up to the room, for the two of them.

They left an hour before midnight, in the Buick, O swathed in a great brown mountaineer's cape and wearing wooden clogs on her feet. Natalie, in a black sweater and slacks, was holding her chain, the leather strap of which was attached to the leather bracelet Natalie was wearing on her right wrist. Sir Stephen was driving. The moon was almost full, and illuminated the road with large snowlike spots, also illuminating the trees and houses of the villages through which they passed, leaving everything else as black as India ink. Here and there, groups of people were still clustered, even at this hour, on the thresholds of streetside doors, and they could feel the people's curiosity aroused by the passage of that closed car (Sir Stephen had not lowered the top). Some dogs were barking. On the side of the road bathed in moonlight, the olive trees looked like silver clouds floating six feet above the ground, and the cypresses like black feathers. There was nothing real about this country, which night had turned into make-believe, nothing except the smell of sage and lavender. The road continued to climb, but the same warm layer of air still lay heavy over the earth. O slipped her cape down off her shoulders. She couldn't be seen, there was not a soul left in sight.

Ten minutes later, having skirted a forest of green oak on the crest of a hill, Sir Stephen slowed down before a long wall into which was cut a porte-cochere, which opened at the approach of the car. He parked in some forecourt as they were closing the gate behind him, then got out and helped Natalie and O out, first having ordered O to leave her cape and clogs in the car.

The door he pushed open revealed a cloister with Renaissance arcades on three sides, the fourth side being an extension of the flagstone court of the cloister proper. A dozen couples were dancing on the terrace and in the courtyard, a few women with very low-cut dresses and some men in white dinner jackets were seated at small tables lighted by candlelight; the record player was in the left-hand gallery, and a buffet table had been set up in the gallery to the right.

The moon provided as much light as the candles, though, and when it fell full upon O, who was being pulled forward by her black little shadow, Natalie, those who noticed her stopped dancing, and the men got to their feet. The boy near the record player, sensing that something was happening, turned around and, taken completely aback, stopped the record. O had come to a halt; Sir Stephen, motionless two steps behind her, was also waiting.

The Commander dispersed those who had gathered around O and had already called for torches to examine her more closely.

"Who is she," they were saying, "who does she belong to?"

"You, if you like," he replied, and he led O and Natalie over to a corner of the terrace where a stone bench covered with cushions was set against a low wall.

When O was seated, her back against the wall, her hands lying on her knees, with Natalie on the ground to the left of her feet, still holding onto the chain, he turned around to them. O's eyes searched for Sir Stephen, and at first could not find him. Then she sensed his presence, reclining on a chaise longue at the other corner of the terrace. He was able to see her, she was reassured. The music had begun again, the dancers were dancing again. As they danced, one or two couples moved over in her direction, as though by accident at first, then one of the couples dropped the pretense and, with the woman leading the way, marched boldly over. O stared at them with eyes that, beneath her plumage, were darkened with bister, eyes opened wide like the eyes of the nocturnal bird she was impersonating, and the illusion was so extraordinary that no one thought of questioning her, which would have been the most natural thing to do, as though she were a real owl, deaf to human language, and dumb.

From midnight till dawn, which began to lighten the eastern sky at about five, as the moon waned and descended toward the west, people came up to her several times, and some even touched her, they formed a circle around her several times and several times they parted her knees and lifted the chain, bringing with them one of those two-branched candlesticks of Provençal earthenware —and she could feel the flames from the candles warming the inside of her thighs—to see how she was attached.

There was even one drunken American who, laughing, grabbed her, but when he realized that he had seized a fistful of flesh and the chain which pierced her, he suddenly sobered up, and O saw his face fill with the same expression of horror and contempt that she had seen on the face of the girl who had given her a depilatory; he turned and fled.

There was another girl, very young, a girl with bare shoulders and a choker of pearls around her neck, wearing one of those white dresses young girls wear to their first ball, two tea-scented roses at her waist and a pair of golden slippers on her feet, and a boy made her sit down next to O, on her right. Then he took her hand and made her caress O's breasts, which quivered to the touch of the cool, light fingers, and touch her belly, and the chain, and the hole through which it passed, the young girl silently. did as she was bid, and when the boy said he planned to do the same thing to her, she did not seem shocked. But even though they thus made use of O, and even though they used her in this way as a model, or the subject of a demonstration, not once did anyone ever speak to her directly. Was she then of stone or wax, or rather some creature from another world, and did they think it pointless to speak to her? Or didn't they dare?

It was only after daybreak, after all the dancers had left, that Sir Stephen and the Commander, awakening Natalie who was asleep at O's feet, helped O to her feet, led her to the middle of the courtyard, unfastened her chain and removed her mask and, laying her back upon a table, possessed her one after the other.

In a final chapter, which has been suppressed, O returned to Roissy, where she was abandoned by Sir Stephen.

There exists a second ending to the story of O, according to which O, seeing that Sir Stephen was about to leave her, said she would prefer to die. Sir Stephen gave her his consent.

Selected Grove Press Paperbacks

E237   ALLEN, DONALD M. (Ed.) / The New American Poetry: 1945-1960 / $5.95

B181   ANONYMOUS / A Man With A Maid / $1.95

B334   ANONYMOUS /My Secret Life / $2.45

B155   ANONYMOUS / The Pearl / $2.95

B383   ARSAN, EMMANUELLE / Emmanuelle II / $1.95

E425   BARAKA, IMAMU AMIRI (LeRoi Jones) / The Baptism and The Toilet / $2.45

E96   BECKETT, SAMUEL / Endgame / $1.95

B78   BECKETT, SAMUEL / Three Novels (Molloy, Malone Dies, The Unnamable / $3.95

E33   BECKETT, SAMUEL / Waiting for Godot / $1.95

B79   BEHAN, BRENDAN / The Quare Fellow and The Hostage: Two Plays / $2.95

B186   BERNE, ERIC / Games People Play / $1.95

B386   BERNE, ERIC / Transactional Analysis in Psychotherapy / $1.95

E417   BIRCH, CYRIL WITH KEENE, DONALD (Eds.) /Anthology of Chinese Literature, Volume 1: From Early Times to the Fourteenth Century / $4.95

E584   BIRCH, CYRIL (Ed.) / Anthology of Chinese Literature, Volume 2: From the 14th Century to the Present Day / $4.95

E368   BORGES, JORGE LUIS / Ficciones / $2.95

B283   BRAUTIGAN, RICHARD / A Confederate General From Big Sur / $1.95

B120   BRECHT, BERTOLT / Galileo / $1.95

B108   BRECHT, BERTOLT / Mother Courage and Her Children / $1.95

B333   BRECHT, BERTOLT / The Threepenny Opera / $1.75

B115   BURROUGHS, WILLIAM S. / Naked Lunch / $1.95

E717   CLURMAN, HAROLD (Ed.) Seven Plays of the Modern Theater / $6.95 (Waiting for Godot by Samuel Beckett, The Quare Fellow by Brendan Behan, A Taste of Honey by Shelagh Delaney, The Connection by Jack Gelber, The Balcony by Jean Genet, Rhinoceros by Eugene Ionesco and The Birthday Party by Harold Pinter)

E190   CUMMINGS, E. E. / Selected Poems / $1.95

E344   DURRENMATT, FRIEDRICH / The Visit / $2.95

B342   FANON, FRANTZ / The Wretched of the Earth / $1.95

E130   GENET, JEAN / The Balcony / $2.95

E208	GENET, JEAN / The Blacks: A Clown Show / $2.95
B382	GENET, JEAN / Querelle / $2.95
B306	HERNTON, CALVIN C. / Sex and Racism in America / $2.95
E101	IONESCO, EUGENE / Four Plays (The Bald Soprano, The Lesson, The Chairs, and Jack, or The Submission) / $2.95
E259	IONESCO, EUGENE / Rhinoceros and Other Plays / $1.95
E216	KEENE, DONALD (Ed.) / Anthology of Japanese Literature; From the Earliest Era to the Mid-Nineteenth Century / $4.95
E573	KEENE, DONALD (Ed.) / Modern Japanese Literature / $5.95
B300	KEROUAC, JACK / The Subterraneans / $1.50
B9	LAWRENCE, D. H. / Lady Chatterley's Lover / $1.95
B373	LUCAS, GEORGE / American Graffiti / $1.50
B146	MALCOLM X / The Autobiography of Malcolm X / $1.95
B326	MILLER, HENRY / Nexus / $2.95
B100	MILLER, HENRY / Plexus / $2.95
B325	MILLER, HENRY / Sexus / $3.95
B10	MILLER, HENRY / Tropic of Cancer / $1.95
B59	MILLER, HENRY / Tropic of Capricorn / $1.95
E636	NERUDA, PABLO / Five Decades: Poems 1925-1970 / $5.95
E359	PAZ, OCTAVIO / The Labyrinth of Solitude: Life and Thought in Mexico / $3.95
E315	PINTER, HAROLD / The Birthday Party and The Room / $2.95
E411	PINTER, HAROLD / The Homecoming / $1.95
B202	REAGE, PAULINE / The Story of O / $1.95
B323	SCHUTZ, WILLIAM C. / Joy / $1.95
B313	SELBY, HUBERT JR. / Last Exit to Brooklyn / $1.95
E618	SNOW, EDGAR / Red Star Over China / $4.95
B319	STOPPARD, TOM / Rosencrantz and Guildenstern Are Dead / $1.95
E219	WATTS, ALAN W. / The Spirit of Zen: A Way of Life, Work and Art in the Far East / $2.95

GROVE PRESS, INC.,
196 West Houston St., New York, N.Y. 10014